WILTSHIRE, D.   F

The tears of Autumn   KCS

12. FEB 09. Damson		
12. MAR 09.		
0 2 APR 2009 Saul		
1 2 APR 2012		
Mc Caughan Leanard perkins		

This item is to be returned or renewed on or before the latest date
above. It may be borrowed for a further period if not in demand.
To renew items call in or phone any Warwickshire library, or renew
on line at www.warwickshire.gov.uk/wild

Discover • Imagine • Learn • *with libraries*

www.warwickshire.gov.uk/libraries

Warwickshire
County Council

SPECIAL MESSAGE TO READERS

This book is published under the auspices of

THE ULVERSCROFT FOUNDATION

(registered charity No. 264873 UK)

Established in 1972 to provide funds for research, diagnosis and treatment of eye diseases. Examples of contributions made are: —

A Children's Assessment Unit at Moorfield's Hospital, London.

●

Twin operating theatres at the Western Ophthalmic Hospital, London.

●

A Chair of Ophthalmology at the Royal Australian College of Ophthalmologists.

●

The Ulverscroft Children's Eye Unit at the Great Ormond Street Hospital For Sick Children, London.

You can help further the work of the Foundation by making a donation or leaving a legacy. Every contribution, no matter how small, is received with gratitude. Please write for details to:

**THE ULVERSCROFT FOUNDATION,
The Green, Bradgate Road, Anstey,
Leicester LE7 7FU, England.
Telephone: (0116) 236 4325**

**In Australia write to:
THE ULVERSCROFT FOUNDATION,
c/o The Royal Australian and New Zealand
College of Ophthalmologists,
94-98 Chalmers Street, Surry Hills,
N.S.W. 2010, Australia**

David Wiltshire qualified as a dental surgeon from University College Hospital, London. He served his National Service as a dental officer in Aden and Singapore before returning to England. He is married with three children and six grandchildren and lives in Bedford.

THE TEARS OF AUTUMN

It is 1938. For two couples honeymooning in Sorrento, the future is uncertain. When Biff and Rosemary Banks meet Konrad and Anna von Riegner they become friends. Biff is a pilot in the RAF and Konrad an *Oberleutnant-zur-See* in the German *Kriegsmarine*. Together they tour the Amalfi coast, and visit the ruins at Pompeii. As they part, swearing undying friendship, they resolve to meet again in a year's time. Yet eleven months later their countries and their friendship are torn apart by a war that lasts for six years. At the end of it, will their friendship have survived?

DAVID WILTSHIRE

◆

THE TEARS OF AUTUMN

ULVERSCROFT
Leicester

First published in Great Britain in 2007 by
Robert Hale Limited
London

First Large Print Edition
published 2008
by arrangement with
Robert Hale Limited
London

British Library CIP Data

Wiltshire, David, *1935 –*
    The tears of Autumn.—Large print ed.—
    Ulverscroft large print series: general fiction
    1. Friendship—Fiction 2. Fraternization—Fiction
    3. World War, *1939 –1945*—Fiction
    4. Large type books
    I. Title
    823.9′14 [F]

    ISBN 978–1–84782–407–3

Published by
F. A. Thorpe (Publishing)
Anstey, Leicestershire

Set by Words & Graphics Ltd.
Anstey, Leicestershire
Printed and bound in Great Britain by
T. J. International Ltd., Padstow, Cornwall

This book is printed on acid-free paper

For my Mother and Father's generation

Author's Note

My thanks to Richard Banks, High Sheriff of Bedfordshire 2006–2007, and his wife Sue, for the inspiration for this book during the service for Her Majesty's Judges in the county, at the parish church of St Paul, Bedford, 25 September 2006.

Nothing except a battle lost can be half so melancholy as a battle won.

The Duke of Wellington

1

He looked up at the stained-glass window. Through the little panes the sun was falling in dusty rays onto the flagstones of the church, the patches of reds, blues and greens shimmering as a leafy tree outside moved in a gentle breeze.

It had been just like that twenty years ago for his service. His gaze moved to a side wall, at the memorial plaques to long-gone bishops and other dead worthies, and from there ascended to the laid-up colours of the local regiments, some dirty and shot-torn in battles long forgotten.

His eyes alighted on the faded blue Colour with its Union Flag in one corner, and red, white and blue rondel in the centre, placed there when the bomber station five miles out of town was finally closed in 1946.

It had been his old service.

His attention came back to the lines of chairs. They were filled up now, the women mostly in hats of all shapes and sizes, some little more than a few skimpy feathers, others so large-brimmed that he couldn't see their owners' faces.

The men were mostly in suits or blazers, with the odd dark-blue number one uniform with Sam Browne, and red stripes down the trouser-legs, dotted amongst them.

Not a badly turned-out bunch.

He was seated near the front and to the right of the congregation. The first few rows of chairs were empty, awaiting the main participants in the annual ceremony that had been going on for 1,000 years. His attention went to the lady sitting all alone in the front row to the left, just one empty chair beside her.

She was very beautiful. He smiled: *almost* as beautiful as his wife when she had sat there.

The cry 'All Stand' rang out. Everybody rose, the man to his right helping him shakily to his eighty-eight-year-old feet.

Led by the mace bearer, the procession of civic dignitaries, the mayor in his ermine-trimmed robe with tricorn hat under his arm, followed by officers of the county and borough with chains hanging from their shoulders, solemnly took their seats.

After the civic procession there was a slight pause while they remained standing, then the crucifer headed the church procession. The choir came first, then the representatives of all the religious faiths of the town. Last of all the church wardens led the Right Reverend Thomas Fullwood, bishop of the diocese, and his chaplain to their seats in the nave.

Everybody sat down again. He loved the pageantry and the feeling of continuity that this ceremony gave. It had been going on since Saxon times — as his wife had gleefully pointed out when he had tried on his silk hose and breeches, ruffle and velvet jacket that dated from the eighteenth century. He smiled as he remembered joking about his sword, and the time when his name had been 'pricked' by Her Majesty when he had been put forward for the office — a tradition inaugurated by her namesake when apparently a quill was not at hand when the petition was presented to her, and she had used a dagger.

Ah, how his wife would have loved being here today. His throat started to ache. She had died a few months ago, and as he was a past holder of the office, would have been invited to attend today beside him. Further thought was interrupted as a fanfare of trumpets rang out.

Led by the vicar of St Paul's, the four purple-robed and bewigged crown court judges were followed by the high sheriffs of surrounding counties, then the coroner, the under sheriff, the chief constable, the

3

chaplain and, bringing up the rear, the man whose service this was. He joined his waiting wife as he had done twenty years before.

They remained standing as the high sheriff's service for Her Majesty's judges in the county commenced with the processional hymn to the tune of *Hanover*.

Later, after the readings given by the incumbent's children, the congregation stood to sing. The hymn was one of his favourites. His voice was thinner than it used to be, but he sang with gusto.

We plough the fields and scatter, the good seed on the land.

Very appropriate he thought. The man was a farmer and seed merchant, and he noticed in the programme that it was being sung to *Wir pflügen*, the setting by J.A.P. Schültz.

That too, would have pleased his wife.

After another hymn and prayers, the Bishop ascended to the pulpit, and preached on the need for everyone, the judges included — and perhaps *especially* them, to remember that they would one day all stand before the judgment-seat of God.

He began to think of his war. He'd killed: sometimes women and children, there could be no getting away from that fact. The

4

innocent had been caught up and ensnared by the evil that had been at the heart of the darkness that they had fought in order to reach Churchill's 'sunny uplands'.

He'd been so lost in his own thoughts that it came as a shock when another fanfare heralded the need to stand and sing the National Anthem. The service was finished. With them still standing the crucifer led out the choir and the church procession, then the mace-bearer and the civic dignitaries, and lastly the high sheriff's party including his wife, led by the vicar of St Paul's.

It was over for another year.

Across the road at the town hall, drinks were dispensed to the large crowd that grew increasingly noisy as the wine was consumed.

Several friends and acquaintances came up to him to shake his hand. In the end his legs couldn't hold out any longer and he had to sit down on a chair set against the wall. His mind began to drift again. It was at a do somewhat like this that he had first met Rosemary.

It was in the mess one summer, pre-war evening. Of course, before that there had been all the thrill of leaving school and going to Cranwell. He'd already been infected by the bug of flying when a friend of his father had taken him up. To this day he wasn't sure whether the man was just naturally wild, or had his father asked him to try and put him off because he wanted his son to join him in the family engineering business.

After a succession of spins, loops and rolls he'd set foot on terra firma again, even more in love with flying than before. He was just one of a generation of young men for whom, in the thirties, the lure and excitement of the skies was overpowering.

So in the autumn of 1937 he entered Cranwell as an officer cadet, and after passing out as a pilot officer, the lowest of the low, he'd been sent on his preliminary flying training course comprising twenty-five hours of dual instruction and a further twenty-five hours solo. The aircraft was an all-metal Blackburn B2 biplane, and where he had expected to be sitting behind the instructor in a separate cockpit in the usual way, he was surprised to find that they were sitting side by side. His instructor was a Flight Lieutenant Johnson who, after eleven hours and twenty minutes of taxiing, flying straight and level, taking off and climbing into the wind, turns, spinning and stall recovery, spent a final twenty minutes with him doing circuits and bumps, then climbed out of the cockpit and told him to do a circuit and land on his own.

To begin with it was unnerving, that empty

seat beside him, but once he was up in the air, over the patchwork fields of England, he felt a glorious freedom. He made it down without incident.

He'd soloed.

There followed more instruction, including aerobatics, side-slipping, instrument flying and finally a solo cross-country flight.

When his assessment came through it spoke of above average, but with a tendency to be rigid. But it was good enough.

His mother and father attended his 'Wings Ceremony', and when his name was called 'Pilot Officer Jack Banks', he marched smartly up to the Air Commodore, saluted, was presented with his wings, said something that he couldn't later recall, before taking one step back, throwing up a snappy salute, turning, and marching off.

He was conscious that his mother and father were in the audience, and felt immensely proud — and mature.

They'd brought his sister who had a friend with her. Before the ceremony he hadn't seen any of them; he'd been too busy with all the others making sure he was turned out immaculately, and it was only later, in the mess as drinks were served by stewards dressed in white jackets, that he had set eyes on his sister's friend — and all the excitement of the day seemed to pale into insignificance. As he took her white-cotton-gloved hand and looked into her wide blue eyes he felt as if he'd just pushed the stick forward and the pit of his stomach had come up into his mouth. She was so beautiful: slim and elegant in a belted summer dress that showed off her tiny waist. She wore a simple wide-brimmed hat with a silk scarf tied around it and trailing down her back. A few curls of blonde hair framed her oval face, with its little turned-up nose and red lips. Jack Banks was smitten.

'How do you do, Miss . . . ?'

He couldn't take his eyes off her as his voice tailed away.

'This is Rosemary,' chuckled his sister, and to her, 'And this is my *big* brother, Jack.'

It was a joke between them, since he was only five foot nine and a half inches tall, to his sister's five foot eight — without her heels. But he was powerfully built, and boxed and played at scrum half both at school and now in the RAF.

Rosemary smiled, little lines radiating out from those glorious eyes.

He continued holding on to her and grinning like an idiot.

'Jack.'

It was his laughing sister, nodding at his hand.

'Oh, sorry.'

Embarrassed he took it away, but kept his eyes on her. Rosemary said: 'Congratulations, you must be very pleased.'

He loved her voice. His own was, to his annoyance, more of a croak.

'Oh, it's fine.'

Another pilot officer started to edge past, accidentally coming between them. The man's interest in Rosemary was obvious, but he said over his shoulder: 'Sorry, Biff.' Still looking at her he moved on into the crowd.

She put her head quizzically on one side. 'Biff?'

He shuffled his feet in embarrassment.

'My nickname.'

Her pearly-white teeth were exposed as she laughed. 'But why Biff?'

'Rhymes with Banks — as in Biffer Banks.'

'Is that all?'

Sheepishly he said: 'I've had some success in the boxing ring.'

'Oh.' She looked a little concerned.

Quickly he explained. 'Only amateur stuff — did it at school — we had to, and you know what boys are — hence Biffer.'

'Have you ever knocked anybody out?'

Worried that he would give the wrong answer, the one that would displease her the most, he hesitated before answering sheepishly.

'Well — just the once.'

She looked at him from under the brim of her hat and raised one eyebrow. 'I thought that sort of thing didn't happen in school boxing.'

'It didn't.'

He realized that he had to explain when she continued to look quizzically at him.

Jack Banks felt quite unnerved by this girl. Every little move she made captivated him.

'Well — it was only a few months ago — against the Navy — a stoker actually.'

Her eyes widened.

'Gosh, they're quite tough, aren't they?'

He nodded. 'Yes — we lost four bouts to one.' Modestly he added, 'It's because I'm a southpaw really. I just caught him with a lucky punch.'

When he saw the concerned look on her face he added hurriedly: 'He was only out for a few seconds, just dazed, really.'

He didn't tell her that it had been a real slugging match and he'd been losing on points, aching and winded by very severe punishment to his body. So when the opportunity came he took it — brutally. His uppercut had slammed home, snapping the man's head back. His body had folded up like a puppet with the strings cut. The packed hangar had gone wild.

And so 'Biffer' — and thence the diminutive 'Biff' had been born once again and he knew that in the Air Force he would always be called it and was resigned to the fact that probably it would stick for ever.

'Can I get you another drink?'

He nodded at her nearly empty glass.

She looked at it herself before seeming to make up her mind. 'I'd like something non-alcoholic if that's possible?'

'Of course.' He caught the attention of one of the mess stewards who offered an orange squash on his tray.

His sister, who had seen the interest her brother had in her new friend whom she'd met when she had joined a solicitor's office in town, now decided to tease him — and her — because she knew enough about Rosemary to see that she was quite taken by Jack.

'Now then, you two, don't forget the rest of us, will you.'

Both of them went bright red, so much so that Elizabeth Banks regretted drawing attention to them, and tried to change the subject.

'Are you coming home this weekend, brother mine?'

'Yes, of course. I've got two weeks' leave before I start the next course.'

His sister doubted that he had intended to

come home straight away, at least, not ten minutes ago. He probably would have been going off with some crowd on a cricket or rowing tour.

She smiled cunningly. 'That's good. Would you partner me then at the Peacocks? They're having a tennis party on the Saturday.'

Just then his mother and father emerged from the crowd.

'Darling, there you are.' His mother, despite the warmth of the day, was in a grey suit and a little blue hat with a net that covered her eyes, and a fox-fur stole around her shoulders, the fox's head and eyes looking dolefully at him.

'Squadron Leader Holmes has been most kind to us. He thinks you might be going to Duxford, dear.'

He groaned. 'Oh mother, you haven't been bothering him, have you?'

'Certainly not. Don't be so sensitive. Father — tell him.'

His father, dressed in a dark-blue blazer and a cravat in the regimental colours of the Royal Dublin Fusiliers — he'd served at Gallipoli in the slaughter that had been 'V' beach — cleared his throat and gave a twitch of his small moustache. 'Your mother's been at her most charming, Jack. Had the squadron leader eating out of her hand.'

That he could well imagine. He had always been aware of her good looks, and when they came to take him home at the end of school terms, he'd been conscious of the other boys and some of the masters showing off in front of her.

And now he had met a girl and he was the one in thrall to a woman's beauty.

'Sorry,' he mumbled.

She put a hand on his arm.

'Nothing to be sorry about dear. I'm so proud of you.' She turned to the girls. 'I see you've met Rosemary.' There was a twinkle in her eyes. She had guessed that her son would find his sister's new friend attractive.

Elizabeth piped up. 'I've just asked Jack if he'll come home this weekend and join the tennis party at the Peacocks on Saturday — isn't that so, Jack? What do you say?'

He looked at Rosemary.

'Will you be there?'

The blue eyes twinkled mischievously.

'Oh, yes, most definitely.'

His sister laughed at him as his face showed his delight.

'Don't be flattered, Biff,' she said 'Biff' with heavy emphasis, 'Rosemary's surname is Peacock.'

He must have looked so crestfallen that Rosemary took pity on him and said: 'My mixed doubles partner can't make it, and Elizabeth tells me you're enthusiastic, if not very talented. Would you consider partnering me?'

Would he!

'Of course — it would be a pleasure.'

'Good.'

In mock shock Elizabeth said to Rosemary, 'Oh, you little toad, I asked him first.'

He spent the rest of the reception looking at her, being moonstruck, as his sister said, and every time some of his fellow officers crowded in he grew terribly jealous, afraid he'd lose her.

At last his father said it was time to leave.

'I'll see you on Saturday then, Miss Peacock.'

'Please — call me Rosemary.'

He did so. 'Rosemary.' It sounded wonderful.

She smiled. 'We're starting at eleven and there's luncheon and high tea. We'll be on third, I think. We can have a knock-up on the back court first.'

'Right.'

She held out her hand.

'Goodbye — and congratulations again.'

He took the slim gloved hand.

'Thank you. I'll do my best on Saturday.'

She gave him a smile, eyes twinkling.

'I'm sure you will.'

His mother suddenly enveloped him in a hug and kissed him on both cheeks, and his father followed with a fine handshake and an affectionate pat on the shoulder.

'Well done, my boy. We knew you would do it.'

Which was more than he had thought at one point. His sister gave him a peck on the cheek as well, and whispered in his ear.

'Rosemary's a good friend. You behave yourself, now — no messing her around.'

He didn't really know what she meant, but he went bright red all the same and snorted: 'Of course, sis. What do you take me for?'

His sister shook her head.

'A man, Jack — at last.'

He went with them to the car, a large Austin Fourteen. His father was driving, mother seated beside him, the two girls in the back, their faces framed by their hats inside the darker interior of the car.

They all waved and he did his best to concentrate on everyone, but really, he only had eyes for Rosemary.

As the RAF personnel guided the cars out of the field he stood there, just able to see the corner of her hat through the small back window. Suddenly the brim moved, and he caught a fleeting glimpse of her face. It thrilled him no end — she *had* looked back.

A couple of his fellow students were passing by. One of them, a bit of a toff who had been at Harrow and Oxford before joining the Air Force said: 'Nice looker, Banks. Too tall for you, though.' It hit a raw nerve.

He swung around, fists bunching up. 'Careful, De Vere, you might find yourself on the deck.'

Despite being six foot two the flash of apprehension in De Vere's eyes was very satisfying.

All the same, Jack was upset. It was true that Rosemary was the same height as his sister, and could look him in the eye, and would be taller with high heels. He cheered up. She didn't seem to care. De Vere drawled again.

'Steady old boy — no offence meant.'

Jack grinned, feeling better.

'None taken — *old* boy.'

Later that night they all got hopelessly drunk on a mixture of champagne, gin and whisky and played British Bulldog inside the mess. A lot of furniture got broken, and Jack ruefully contemplated the thought that his mess bill could be pretty steep, he might even have to ask his father for a loan.

★ ★ ★

'Biff'

He suddenly came to as a woman shook his arm. 'Biff.'

He looked at her blankly for a moment and then realized it was the wife of his friend who had been the town's mayor when he had been the chairman of the local bench.

'Biff, we should start going upstairs for the lunch.' She helped him to his feet and they made their way slowly to the lift that took them up to the dining room. Not everybody was invited to the lunch, so they had been asked, as always, to make their way discreetly and to be in place by 12.45. When they entered the room there were lots of round tables with bright white cloths and place settings, with flowers decorating the centre of each table.

Slowly the room filled up, many people coming over to say hello to him.

The judges and their wives gathered around one table, the judges dressed now in their ordinary suits. Eventually the high sheriff and his wife took their positions, and it was announced that the bishop would say grace.

After that they all sat down and immediately the noise in the room rose.

As white wine was poured into his glass it caught the sun . . .

★ ★ ★

He drew the Singer sports car on to the gravelled drive of the large house, past the fountain, where the sun was glinting on the bubbling water. Several other cars were parked around the house. He pulled on the handbrake, turned off the engine and jumped out without opening the door, collecting his racket and bag from the back seat. He was dressed in his white flannels, with his striped cricket blazer and cravat.

The big front door was shut, but he could hear laughter and the sound of balls being whacked coming from around the side of the house.

He made his way along the stone path. Disappointed, he had had no idea it was going to be such a big do: there were at least thirty-five people sitting or standing outside the pavilion situated beyond two grass courts. Another court lay to the side.

Aimlessly and a little deflated he mingled with the crowd, watching two mixed doubles matches going on, until a voice called out:

'Biff — over here.'

He turned, and there she was, wearing a brilliant white tennis skirt, quite short, at least compared to those of the ladies who played with his mother, and a top with straps made of metal figures of eight, leaving her shoulders bare.

Her blonde hair was held back off her face by a bandeau. If anything she looked better than before: something he wouldn't have thought possible.

He made his way towards her, irritated that she was surrounded by three young bucks.

'Hello there, sorry I'm late.'

She smiled, and his heart soared.

'Better late than never. Have you met my brother?'

He dragged his attention from her to one of the men, feeling better and a little ashamed of himself. He held out his hand. 'No, I'm Jack Banks.'

She chipped in, grinning, 'But they call him Biff.'

Her brother shook his hand, and chuckled.

'How do you do — Biff. I'm John Peacock. These are a couple of friends of mine.'

He shook hands with them as they introduced themselves.

His jealousy came back again as he saw Rosemary looking admiringly at one of them, called Robert, who was telling the crowd about his time in Australia. Eventually he butted in rather awkwardly.

'I've brought my racket.'

He waved it around like some schoolboy,

realizing he was being rather gauche.

They all looked at him for a moment, then the men exchanged sly grins as Rosemary said with a throaty chuckle: 'Keen aren't we? All right come on Biff, let's see how good you are.'

Miserably he trailed after her as she made her way to the third court. What a fool he was making of himself.

Two people had just finished having a knock-up. They stopped and talked to her as he waited like an idiot.

Then she turned to him and said: 'I'll take the other end.' With that she skipped off. Surreptitiously, he couldn't take his eyes off her flapping skirt and slim legs.

They knocked the ball sedately back and forth for a while.

She moved freely, reaching his shots with ease, her backhand particularly accurate.

When the ball hit the net and dropped back on his side for the fourth time she said: 'Shall we have a game?'

He picked up the ball.

'If you like, though I'm not sure I'm going to give you much of a run for your money.'

'You serve first,' she ordered. He dutifully took up his position on the baseline, bouncing the ball several times before throwing it up and whacking it — straight into the net. Rosemary, who had been standing ready to receive, straightened up and relaxed, bouncing up and down on her toes before resuming her stance.

This time he didn't hit the ball with anything like the strength of the first, and it sailed over the net — to be seized on by Rosemary who slammed it straight back up the court. He ruefully made for the opposite corner.

She beat him in the end 6–3 6–4, running up to the net with her hand held out.

'Thank you — and thank you for really trying.'

He took it, finding it slim and cool, but she had quite hard skin on her palm and fingers. It was something she was aware of, perhaps embarrassed by, as she said quickly: 'Comes from riding — I take care of my own horses.' She pulled off the bandeau that she had put on to hold her hair off her face and eyes.

'Come on, let's get some Pimms.'

He walked beside her.

'What did you mean — thank you for really trying?'

'Oh, it's just some young men think it's ungallant to beat a woman.'

He pulled a wry face.

'I wouldn't think they could do that very often with you.'

She smiled at him as they found the towels and put their rackets into their wooden presses to keep them from bending out of shape.

'You have no idea how they think it's going to make them more attractive to me. I like you because you did your damned best, and with a bit of coaching you would easily overpower me.'

Her use of 'overpower' left him reeling at the thought.

'Here we are.' They paused by a waitress bearing a silver salver, and took tall glasses of Pimms with an extra mint-leaf decorating the edge.

Rosemary took hers out and threw it casually away.

'Cheers.'

He responded.

'Now, let's go and sit over there, and you can tell me more about your flying. It sounds very exciting.'

As they made their way to a white wrought-iron seat set deeper into the rhododendrons he couldn't believe his luck.

They were observed by her brother and a couple of friends, one of whom said: 'Rosemary seems to have taken a shine to him.'

John nodded, and shook his head in mock horror.

'He won't stand a chance if she likes him.'
And like him she did.

As Biff, at first stumbling and trying to be as modest as possible as he explained about flying, and then got more and more excited, she quietly observed him: his face, his movements, the gesture of his strong-looking hands. Her mind was elsewhere as she pretended to understand about how wonderful it was to be soaring in and out of clouds as the fields and trees and hills of England passed by far below.

In reality, she was thinking of his hands on her, of that mouth, strong, slightly cruel-looking, pressed against her own.

'So, I'm going to be flying Hawker Harts now. I should get a squadron posting soon — when the training finally comes to an end.'

She came back from her flight of fancy with a rush. 'Oh, really?'

Biff had a vague awareness that perhaps she had not been wholly listening. If he was disappointed he soon cheered up as she said: 'Biff, perhaps I could come and visit you some time — at your airfield?'

He felt almost giddy with excitement. She was wanting to see him again.

'Yes — yes, I'd like that very much. We do have open days, there is one coming in a couple of weeks' time.'

'Oh good. Will you be flying?'

He swallowed, knowing he more than likely wouldn't be, at least not solo or anything. If they did a mass formation flypast, that would be the best he could hope for. He tried to sound nonchalant. 'It's possible — we don't know the programme yet.'

The programme yet . . .

★ ★ ★

'Biff, have you seen the menu.'

His female dining companion on his right held the card out for him. 'It's got one of your favourites — lamb chops.' He laughed with her. It was well known that Biff liked good plain English cooking — and mutton was his favourite: the stew.

The first course was served, salmon, and conversation around the table grew. He was careful, wary of bones: his eyesight was getting poorer every year.

'Biff, what do you do with yourself these days?'

She was trying to be nice, he knew, but today was a rare treat, and he didn't want to be reminded how routine his world had become.

'Oh, nothing much. Get on my buggy most mornings, do some shopping, have a coffee,' his eyes twinkled, 'sometimes even a gin and tonic in the Horse and Groom.'

But in reality there were some days when he dreaded getting out of bed. *She* was gone, his pal, his lover for over sixty years, only the occasional visits by his son and daughter had any meaning in his life now.

His daughter had brought him today; she was over on a table of young ones — he gave a grunt: they were all in their forties and fifties with families of their own, but they knew each other from schooldays.

'Oh, you naughty boy you.'

Biff did his best to suppress a wince. God almighty, what was it about getting old that everyone had to patronize you? Then he relented. She was trying to be convivial, and quite honestly was probably finding it hard going sitting beside an old man. They had nothing in common — how could they have? She was no older than his daughter. He was a bit of a dinosaur now, having grown up, experienced a terrible war and been a mature man, all in an age that had radically different values from today.

He smiled, and started to say something, but was dimly aware of the woman frowning.

★　★　★

25

He was strapped into the cockpit of the Hart, the powerful Rolls Royce Kestrel engine at a fast tick-over to prevent the plugs oiling, the whole airframe throbbing and rumbling. Everywhere he looked were the now familiar wires, gauges, copper pipes and brass fittings, but they didn't offer any comfort today. He was on his final check ride. For a brief moment his eyes dropped to the spade-shaped joystick, and the gun-firing button that said 'Safe' and 'Fire'.

How this flight went could well decide which way his career went in the service. He dragged his mind back to the job in hand. The engine sounded throaty and harsh. The vibration was now considerable and the reduction gear of the hefty twin-bladed airscrew clanked and rattled.

Biff brought his goggles down over his eyes, took a deep breath, and waved the chocks away to taxi out.

When he gently eased the throttle open it felt as if the engine was going to tear itself out of the frame. The biplane was solid, fast and powerful, with a long nose with a pointed spinner — a different animal from the other training aircraft he had flown. In fact, it wasn't just a training aircraft, it was also in service with front-line squadrons, of which only a few had been equipped with the new

Hurricanes, even fewer with the Spitfire.

On the grass runway, marked out with lights, he opened the throttle wide and released the brakes.

His shoulders were forced hard back against the metal bucket seat, and he felt as if his cheeks were being dragged back towards his ears. The slipstream blasted the open cockpit as the wheels thumped and thudded over the grass until suddenly it ceased.

He was airborne.

He went through his routine, knowing he was being observed not only from the ground, but by Squadron Leader Forster, aloft and patrolling the skies to one side of the field where he was not permitted to fly.

He'd been at it for twenty minutes when the engine started to miss. Only seconds later it failed completely.

Automatically he went through the forced landing routine that had been drummed into him, and brought the Hart in over a hedge and landed, bouncing somewhat roughly in a field of cows — who stampeded away to the other end.

Biff undid his harness and climbed out on to the wing, tearing his goggles and helmet off in disgust as the squadron leader's aircraft swooped low overhead.

2

'How did it go?'

It was Rosemary, running out to him as he drove the Singer into her drive and up to the house.

He smiled bleakly, and told her what had happened.

She frowned. 'Well, that wasn't your fault, was it — and you did everything correctly, is that right? The aeroplane is not damaged is it?'

Glumly he agreed.

'Come on.' She put her arm through his. 'Come and have a drink.'

He'd been going with Rosemary now for several months. She had come to their open day; but unfortunately he hadn't flown that day, but he had since then buzzed the house a couple of times, risking censure, and she had been present when he had at last taken part in a formation flypast on a visit to a famous air show. He knew they were getting closer when she drove all the way to Hendon in London, where he had landed and was able to meet her in the enclosure for tea. After that they had gone out together regularly to the cinema and picnics and garden parties.

And they had *kissed* and canoodled.

She had hinted several times of how close they had become, and he knew she was expecting him to pop the question soon — something he would have thought inconceivable six months previously. Over-joyed as he was, he wanted to be sure of his place in the Air Force, to finish his training and eventually be in a front-line squadron. It seemed the sensible thing to do before he declared himself.

And now he had gone and messed everything up.

Her father was sitting in his brown leather armchair, smoking his favourite tobacco, Three Nuns, in his brier pipe, and with the *Daily Telegraph* on his lap.

'Hello Biff, how are you?'

'Fine sir — really.'

'Good, good. Rosemary taking care of you?'

'Yes, Father.'

She was already at the drinks cabinet, fixing Biff a large gin, squirting in tonic from the net-cladded Schweppes siphon.

Her father was dressed in his favourite blue cardigan with elbow patches, his feet in old felt slippers. He folded the *Telegraph* back to its front page and then in half again, tapping the paper with a knuckle.

'Seen the headline?'

Biff came over and looked down at it.

'Herr Hitler again?'

'Yes, the Sudetenland Germans are starting to clamour for self-government, and Hitler is making noises about incorporation into the Greater Reich.'

Biff sniffed. 'Not satisfied with Austria then?' He was referring to the *Anschluss* in March and then the making of Austria into a state of the Third Reich the following month.

Rosemary handed him his gin and tonic.

'Daddy?'

Her father looked at his watch, then shrugged.

'Why not.'

To Biff he said: 'What's the talk in your mess?'

'How do you mean, sir?'

'Do they — your senior officers — do they expect war with Germany?'

Biff looked into the sparkling drink in the tumbler he held in both hands. 'Well, I suppose there is a growing realization that we should be better prepared — just in case. We are woefully under strength after the savage cuts of the last few years. Ever since Lord Swinton resigned as Secretary of State for Air they have been very worried.'

'Hmm.' Her father shook his head slowly. 'I pray it never comes. I don't know if the youth of this country are up to it . . . '

Suddenly realizing what he had implied he added hurriedly: 'No offence, Biff. I don't mean the likes of you regulars, I just don't think the ordinary young of today have the same spirit, the same sense of nationhood and Empire that we had. We lost the best of our generation.'

Biff knew that Rosemary's father had served as an infantry officer from the Somme to Passchendaele before he had stopped his 'Blighty one'.

'Surely, that's being a bit hard, isn't it?'

Her father didn't answer, and fortunately her mother came into the room just then.

'Biff, how lovely to see you. Have you just arrived?'

He liked her mother very much.

'Yes, Mrs Peacock.'

'I'll have one of those.' She nodded at his drink as she flopped into a chair opposite her husband, having given him a peck on the top of his head.

'Now, what are you two boys talking about?'

Her father shot a glance at Biff, then said, 'Just current affairs, darling. Politics.'

'Oh, not the prospect of a bloody war again, Frank.'

31

Mr Peacock grinned sheepishly at Biff.

'That's what comes of being married to the same woman for thirty-odd years.'

★ ★ ★

He got the results, and his posting, a week later. Biff had hoped for a fighter squadron. After they had kissed he faced Rosemary in the bar of the tennis club where they'd arranged to meet.

'I'm going to Blenheims.'

'Oh.' She didn't really know what to say. 'That's all right — yes?'

Biff grimaced. 'I had my heart set on a Hurricane or Spitfire squadron — who doesn't, but Blenheims are fast enough. They are two-engined fighter-bombers.'

Rosemary sniffed. 'Sounds jolly good to me. When do you go?'

'I've got three weeks' leave, then it's back here for a day, then I'll be off.'

Rosemary couldn't conceal her disappointment.

'Oh, I shan't see you, then, for weeks?'

Glumly he shook his head. If anybody had told him previously that, when he had eventually finished his training and was about to join a squadron, he would be down in the mouth, he wouldn't have believed it. But he did have one answer to their problem.

He drew in a deep breath, and steeled himself for what he had worried about all day — all week in fact.

'There's a solution.'

Rosemary was sitting on a bar stool. She looked up at him, puzzled, then with a dawning expectancy as he continued to gaze helplessly at her.

'Yes?'

Biff swallowed, audibly.

'We could . . . Well . . . '

With growing excitement she nearly said it for him, but bit her tongue; after all, he was the *man*, he *had* to do it . . . Well, she would give him another twenty seconds.

At last Biff managed:

'Will you marry me?'

'Oh, Biff.' She fell off the stool into his arms and gave him a whopping kiss. 'Of course I will, you big idiot.'

'You will?'

'Yes.'

'That's great.'

For a moment there was a silence, both of them stunned with what had just happened. It was broken at last by Biff apologizing: 'I haven't got a ring.'

Her eyes twinkled.

'Well you can jolly well get one tomorrow

33

morning, you're free now. Is that right?'

He started to feel dizzy.

'Right.'

They went straight home to her parents. It was asking a lot, but they had already decided that they were going to tie the knot as quickly as they could after the banns had been read — that meant three weeks minimum, then as soon as the Air Force would let him have leave — he would find out when, and apply as soon as he arrived on the squadron.

Her mother was knitting, sitting with the standard lamp behind her armchair, turned on even though it was daylight.

Through the french window they could see her father on the terrace.

Mrs Peacock looked up and spoke, without stopping the clicking needles.

'Oh, hello dears, would you like some tea?'

'No mother. One of Daddy's champagnes.'

This time the needles did stop.

★   ★   ★

The lamb was excellent. His appetite was still good, at least, when the food was good. He put his knife and fork together and took a sip of wine.

'Gosh, you were hungry.'

He smiled resignedly. People didn't expect

34

men of his age to clean their plate. On top of that they now lived in a wasteful society. More good food was thrown away than ever before. Somehow, if there was another war — one that threatened these shores, he doubted whether the modern generation would be able to cope. Not like in their day.

Then he thought of what Mr Peacock had said to him all those years ago, about his generation.

He grinned to himself. What goes around comes around.

He was behaving just like Rosemary's father had. But the smile faded at the memory . . .

The room was now a hubbub of voices, as people moved around the tables talking to friends in other parts of the room. Half the diners at his table were gone, but a man slipped into the empty chair beside him.

'Hello, Biff, it's good to see you again.'

It was a friend of his daughter.

She had attended one of the girls-only schools in town, but he had been part of the crowd from the boys' school. Socially they had all mixed together. He was married now to a daughter of a friend, but at one time he had been always in their house. He might have been a son-in-law . . .

He stirred himself, turning in his chair.

'Peter, didn't see you earlier.'

The man sat down sideways on the next chair, elbow on the table.

'No, I wasn't at the church service, or reception. Had to work for my sins.'

Peter was now a surgeon who, after all his training up in town and jobs around the country, had got a consultancy locally.

'Called away, I'm afraid. Jill hasn't forgiven me yet.'

They both grinned. Jill, his wife, was a very strong-willed lady who had probably demanded that there must have been somebody else at 'that bloody place' who could do the job.

'Anyway, how are you keeping?'

Biff pulled a funny face.

'At my age — brilliant.'

Peter chuckled, then glanced around.

'I hear your daughter is here.'

Biff nodded. 'Yes, she's over on table eleven — go over and say hello.'

'I will, I will.'

He suspected that Peter still had a soft spot for her, and he was not surprised. Even though he said it himself, his daughter was a good-looking girl, just like her mother; *very* like her mother.

He could hardly hear Peter as his memories crowded in.

There were a couple of days to go before they got married. Rosemary had persuaded him to get on a horse, not his thing at all, and they had just ridden at a walking pace down a lane. Rosemary didn't dismount as she opened a gate into a field and he eased his horse cautiously through, conscious of all the wide open space suddenly before him. She was just closing it again when out of the corner of his eye he saw the huge maroon locomotive lumbering right beside them, hissing steam as it cruised slowly past, held by a signal to proceed with caution.

His steed must have seen and heard the 'monster' too, for in a flash he was cantering, ears back and flicking, nearly keeping abreast with the engine. Hanging on for dear life, Biff found himself the object of scores of white faces at the windows of the Carlisle-bound express as it slowly overhauled them.

'Wooh, slow down, you bugger.' He pulled on the reins with all his strength, just hearing Rosemary's voice in the distance screaming: 'Keep your heels down,' before the horse stopped dead and he was flying in a completely unaccustomed way.

It all came to an abrupt end as his body hit the ground, flat, and all the air in him came out of every orifice in his body.

By the time Rosemary caught up, dismounting at the run to kneel beside him, the last coach of the now accelerating express, hauled by the *Princess Margaret Rose* was receding out of sight under a bridge.

'Biff — Biff darling, are you all right?'

She was desperately worried.

For the first few seconds he wondered whether he was paralysed for life, unable to move a muscle. Then his lungs started up again and he moved a foot. She stroked his forehead.

'I'm so sorry, darling, I forgot about the railway. My fault, I suppose. I always race the trains. Darling?'

Biff eased himself into an upright position, raised one eyebrow.

'You mean the horse was only doing what you trained it to do?'

'Well, yes, but — '

She gave a little scream as Biff pulled her down over his lap and started to spank the seat of her tightly fitting jodphurs.

'Biff — Biff — stop!'

But when he rolled her over again her face was flushed, eyes hooded.

'Ooh, you're so strong and masterful — just like Errol Flynn.'

With that she flung her arm up around his neck and drew his mouth hard down on to hers.

As they carried on kissing the horses stood nearby quietly grazing, only a drifting layer of smoke marked the passage of the train.

⋆　⋆　⋆

'Are you sure about this honeymoon?'

They were gathered in the drawing room, dressed for dinner. Mr Peacock still stuck to the older ways, which were beginning to change in some trendy new quarters.

It was her mother who spoke, anxious because they had booked their honeymoon in Sorrento, Italy. There and Capri were favourite areas for honeymooners, and Rosemary had set her heart on it. Biff had enquired of his CO and been told that there was no objection.

But in the last few days the Sudetanland question had started to become a crisis again. On 12 September the year before Adolph Hitler had demanded self-determination for the German-speaking area.

Mr Peacock did indeed look serious.

That very day, 23 September, the wireless had informed them that the Prime Minister, Neville Chamberlain, was flying to Munich to see Herr Hitler. He'd made one trip on the fifteenth already.

He shook his head. 'No use denying it's

serious, but you should both be all right in Italy, even though they are allies of the Germans. Mussolini says he wants peace, and is willing to help. I believe he suggested the talks to Herr Hitler.'

Her father went on, obviously trying to reassure himself more than them. 'I've had assurances from the embassy in Rome that in such an unlikely event —— '

Mrs Peacock broke in sharply. 'You didn't say — have you been on to your brother?'

Rosemary's father looked uncomfortable. He had indeed spoken to Charles, who worked in the Foreign Office.

'Well, I wouldn't be doing my job as a father if I didn't look after my daughter right up to the moment she becomes another man's responsibility.'

'Daddy, you're a darling.' Rosemary, in a full length loosely fitting lilac satin dress with a pale voile overskirt, went up on her toes and kissed his cheek.

'So it's all right then?'

He smiled down at her. 'If I was really worried I'd be pressing young Biff here to take you to the cottage in Gloucestershire and let me pick up the bill for the cancellations, I promise you.'

It was the last time Biff and Rosemary would spend an evening together. Biff's posting had turned out to be good after all. The squadron was very friendly, a great bunch of chaps, and the CO had assigned him to a Flight Lieutenant Dickinson, a blunt no-nonsense Yorkshire man who was introducing him, via the squadron Anson, to multi-engined flight. He was going to have a guard of honour, with ten fellow officers in dress uniforms holding their ceremonial swords to form an arch beneath which he and his new wife would walk on leaving the church.

But he had to get through his stag night first. Apparently things could get pretty exciting in the mess — and cause further expense for him.

'So, that's all the details, then. Nothing left to chance.'

Her mother winced. 'Rosemary, never say things like that.'

'Oops, sorry Mummy.'

Rosemary bit her lower lip.

Just then their housekeeper and cook entered the room.

'Dinner is ready when you are, Mrs Peacock.'

'Right — let's go in. I'm famished.'

Mr Peacock held his arm out for his wife who downed the last of her pink gin and slipped her arm through his.

'Lead on, Macduff.'

Biff did the same for Rosemary who whispered: 'Next time we do this we'll be man and wife.'

His stag night was a riot. He ended up naked, with his balls painted with blacklead, and tied to the CO's chair in the latter's office.

Fortunately, although he was there all night — or for what was left of it, he was discovered by the adjutant's clerk when he brought in some early-morning signals to put on the CO's desk. He could hardly walk, he was so stiff, but the effects of an excess of beer and spirits had helped pass the night quite quickly.

The big worry was his privates. Despite repeated washing his anatomy remained a disgusting-looking grey colour. He worried about the wedding night. Would Rosemary actually get to see his tackle? He had no idea really what would happen. He consoled himself that, in the dark, he would get away with it.

He was not flying on his last day — in fact the MO would probably have had a fit if he had examined him, but Dicky Dickinson had made sure he was only occupied with ground school.

That evening he packed. They were having

their first night at the Connaught in London. Next day they would go to Victoria Station and take the boat train to Paris. After a night there at the Ritz they were booked on the Rome Express. The final leg was to Naples and then a local train to Sorrento.

Rosemary was thrilled, and most of her packing was already done. She'd spent the morning riding, galloping her horse across the meadows, even taking a fence. It was as if she had so much energy pent up in every part of her body. Rosemary was a virgin, but it had been a struggle — especially after she had met Biff, and known he was the one for her. A few cads before him knew that she was very sensual and had tried their luck. At the last moment she had always backed out of going all the way. But she had done some naughty things.

Now she was in her bath, lying with foam bubbles all around her. She looked down at the pink tips that were her nipples. Rosemary had the idea that Biff was a bit slow in these matters — a typically British public-schoolboy who had healthy instincts, but who, having never socialized much with girls in his earlier years, was rather afraid of them — or at least of *hurting* them, and who was painfully shy at times.

She lifted her hand up from the water,

second finger and thumb making a circle with a soapy film between. She brought it to her lips and blew very gently. For a moment it ballooned out, then burst with a faint dampness.

She giggled. Just like her hymen — tomorrow night.

Biff ate a hearty breakfast of eggs and bacon in the mess, surrounded at various times by the ten brother officers who were forming the guard of honour. His best man was an old school-chum who had stayed in one of the guest bedrooms.

'Well Biff, this is it.'

He nodded, his mouth full.

'Any second thoughts?'

He swallowed. 'I've never been so sure of anything in my life — except perhaps joining the Air Force.'

James, a man he'd first met in *The Inky*, their prep school, and had had a fight with, thus establishing a lifetime's friendship, grinned, 'That's good because I don't fancy making your apologies after you've absconded.'

Biff grinned. 'Don't worry so much. Just make sure your speech is up to scratch.'

His best man winced. They ate in silence for a while until James spoke again.

'Have you any concerns about going abroad at the moment?'

'You mean this Munich crisis?'

James buttered a piece of toast.

'Yes. War could break out at any time.'

Biff shook his head.

'With Halifax as foreign secretary and Chamberlain as PM, they'll appease him — you can bet on that. Besides . . .'

James raised an eyebrow quizzically.

'Besides what?'

Biff placed his knife and fork together.

'Frankly, we are not in a fit state — at least the Air Force. We need all the time we can to get up to strength.'

3

'Biff, Biff.'

A hand was shaking his arm.

'Biff, do you want the lemon meringue pie?'

He took in the young woman at his side, then looked up at the waitress waiting expectantly with a plate ready to put down before him.

'Oh, yes please.'

People were mostly back at their tables. He couldn't remember saying goodbye to Peter, who wasn't around.

He turned to his dining companion.

'Could I have some water please?'

'Yes, of course.'

She half stood up and reached out for the bottle of spring water. When she got it she poured some into his tumbler. He was feeling very thirsty.

'Thank you, my dear.'

The pie was good, dissolving in his mouth which was just as well as he was beginning to feel full up.

He made some small talk for a while, then sat back as the coffee was poured and little dishes of mints were placed on the table.

He noticed the high sheriff had got up and

was coming his way, albeit stopping to talk to people. Biff guessed what it was: he was going to commiserate with him about the death of his wife; he hadn't seen him since.

Bugger. He could do without that just now. The last thing he wanted was to blub in public, but it could easily happen, even after these weeks.

He took a sip of coffee, finding it already difficult to swallow. His mind wandered back again to 1938. It had been a great wedding, he could still remember that archway of swords, and the young fresh faces of the airmen bearing them, laughing as the bells pealed out with joy.

Even now he could recall their names, like a litany.

Dickinson, Knowles, Stillman, Ormerod, Bowker, Rose, Grace, Hicks, Clark and MacWilliams, the last two both called Paddy since they were Irish.

The reception had been brilliant, with James making a good fist of the best man's speech, leaving him writhing in embarrassment at some of the schoolboy things he'd got up to, especially the time he'd put black soot on all the eyepieces of the binoculars and telescopes at the annual school regatta.

The thrashing he'd received from the headmaster who, an hour before, had looked like a panda, had been exceptional. Happily, in anticipation of what was coming, he'd slipped two slices of ham from the school kitchen under his shorts. It took some of the sting out of the cane, and still made the right noise — as did he.

The good news had been announced on the wireless while they were changing to catch the London train. Agreement had been reached at Munich — no details as yet.

As they stepped into the car taking them to the station, and rice was thrown over them in great handfuls, the whole wedding reception knew the good news. An air of almost hysterical jubilation permeated the gathering.

With loud cheers, and a final rejoinder from Mr Peacock to 'Take care of her now Biff,' they swept away.

Almost immediately the quietness descended and they were left all on their own, the driver on the other side of the Rolls's thick glass screen.

They looked at each other.

She was dressed in a pale silk coat, and wearing a tiny little hat with a net veil that covered her eyes.

Their hands met on the seat. He covered hers and squeezed.

'Hello, Mrs Banks.'

She smiled, and put her head on his shoulder.

'Hello, Mr Banks.'

Most of their luggage, including her trunk, was taken on to Victoria Station. They only retrieved an overnight bag each, which were placed in their room by a porter summoned by the concierge.

Biff tipped him ten bob — way, way, over the odds even by the Connaught's standards, but he was feeling almost light-headed with expectancy.

They had a suite, so they had their own bathroom and separate lavatory.

In the elegantly decorated dining-room they had a light supper; in fact, after the blow-out of the wedding breakfast he wasn't hungry at all.

When the time came at last he coughed and said: 'Perhaps you'd care to go up first? I'll have a last cigar.'

She flashed him a coy look.

'Don't be too long now. Fifteen minutes will be quite enough, or you might find me asleep. It's been a long day.'

With that she pushed back her chair, picked up the keys, gave a little wave of her fingers and left.

Biff went out into the lounge, ordered a brandy and selected a cigar from the humidor held by a waiter.

He stepped out on to the hotel's terrace.

Somewhere he could hear music and a crooner softly singing of love.

All of a sudden he felt very happy. He was married to a beautiful girl, he was a pilot in the Royal Air Force, and he was about to go on honeymoon in a world that at least for the foreseeable future was at peace.

'What more could a man ask for?'

He tapped lightly on the door, but found it was not locked. When he entered the lights were down low, and there was a lovely smell of Chanel No. 5 in the air.

'Rosemary?'

'Come in, darling.'

He closed the door and locked it. Through the half-open bedroom door he could see the bed, but it was only when he eased the door gently open that Rosemary was revealed, sitting up, her creamy white shoulders and neck in contrast to the dark mahogany headboard and the straps of her black-silk nightdress.

Biff took a step towards her.

★ ★ ★

'Hello Biff, old chap, how are you getting along?'

It was the high sheriff in all his finery, black velvet jacket, white shirt with ruffles and cravat, silken breeches and black hose. Each holder of the office had to buy his own formal dress at a cost of several thousands of pounds. His was still in a back bedroom somewhere, together with his sword.

Biff smiled back at him and started to get up to shake hands. 'High Sheriff . . . '

'No, no.' The high sheriff crouched down beside him. 'Just came over to see how you are getting on. Glad you could make it today.'

'Thank you for including me, Richard.'

It was customary for past high sheriffs to be involved, but it was nice to be invited; after all, it had been a good many years since he had held the office.

'I meant to come round but I've been so busy . . . '

Biff nodded. 'I understand.'

The high sheriff and his friends were all one generation, so it was not as if he saw them regularly on a social basis — those days were now long gone. Although he was well known, he was now a lonely old man, left behind really.

They chatted for several minutes before the high sheriff straightened up. 'Right, I'm going off to get comfortable before the speeches. These button flies bring back memories, eh, Biff? Wish I'd gone for the zip option.'

Left on his own again he nodded. Yes, he remembered when his hands were freezing in the war, and it was bloody impossible to do them back up in a hurry, the fingers just didn't work.

Fingers. He remembered cool soft fingers, doing things to him that nobody had ever done before. Rosemary had certainly been a shock. Unfortunately he'd disgraced himself, unable to control his own body. Fortunately, and with the vigour of youth, later in the night he had at last managed to hang on long enough for Rosemary to get involved.

He shook his head in wonder. Nobody ever talked about difficulties in those days. It was all supposed to happen just like that, and also it was the *girl* who was supposed to be apprehensive. He grinned inwardly. In their case it was Rosemary who had certainly taught him a thing or two.

He was aware of the room settling down again and of some of the diners turning their chairs towards the top table. He glanced at the menu card. The judges always spoke first, in this case it was his Honour Judge Richard Gordon.

Biff knew him to be a soft-spoken man, but he had a wicked sense of humour, not always appreciated by the miscreants before him on the bench.

Somewhere, somebody banged a table several times and a loud voice carried in the quietening room.

'Your Grace, lords, ladies and gentlemen, His Honour, Judge Richard Gordon, QC, who will propose the toast to the high sheriff.'

The clapping started all around him.

★ ★ ★

Biff shouldered through the crowds on the platform at Victoria Station, searching the windows of the yellow and brown Pullman cars of the *Golden Arrow* express.

After they had settled into their first class seats he had, much to Rosemary's annoyance, insisted on getting off again to get the papers, the *Daily Telegraph* for him and *Daily Express* for her. She didn't seem to care much about the momentous news scrawled in black on all the newstands: *Peace in Our Time*.

He'd meant to get them as they had followed their porters, with their luggage on barrows, past the W.H. Smith kiosk, but had been distracted by the station announcer's voice echoing incoherently around the glass-and-iron vault of the station roof, just as an engine's safety valve lifted and blasted steam, so that he couldn't hear exactly what was said, but it was something about the Channel. Was it rough? He wasn't a good sailor.

In the event it was to do with workings on

the permanent way to the coast — adding some ten minutes to their journey.

He suddenly saw her, waving in the window of a coach called *Annabel*, steam rising from somewhere beneath, obscuring her for a second.

As he boarded at the end door whistles shrilled on the platform and doors slammed.

He slumped into the seat opposite her and took off his trilby hat, just as the coach gave a lurch forward.

'Phew, that was close.'

Rosemary raised an eyebrow and said sarcastically: 'That would have been fun, wouldn't it? I have a husband for just one night, then he stays in London while I go off to the most romantic city on earth. That's a dangerous way to treat a girl, isn't it?'

He leant forward over the table and kissed her on the tip of her nose.

'Just as long as you behave yourself, Mrs Banks.'

She put the tip of a finger on his forehead and pushed him away.

'Mr Banks, you've started a fire in me that only *you* can put out.'

He went bright red.

All the way down to Dover, through the Kent countryside with its tall hop frames and apple orchards, he read the news. There was a photograph of Mr Chamberlain, stepping off the plane at Heston, waving a piece of paper with apparently Herr Hitler's signature on it.

As he read further it became apparent the Sudetanland was being transferred to Germany. Edvard Beneš, Czechoslovakia's head of state, had protested at the decision, but Neville Chamberlain had told him that Britain would be unwilling to go to war over the issue: after all, they were German-speaking peoples.

Eduard Daladier, the French President had agreed and Mussolini was being praised for setting up the four-power meeting and acting as an 'honest broker'.

Biff gave a little grunt at that. For a start, he hadn't even invited the Russians, who had more of an interest in the region than either France or Britain, they being fellow Slavs.

He read the full statement dated 30 September 1938.

We, the German Führer and Chancellor, and the British Prime Minister, have had a further meeting today and are agreed in recognizing that the question of Anglo German relations is of the first importance for the two countries and for Europe.

We regard the agreement signed last

night, and the Anglo German Naval Agreement, as symbolic of the desire of our two peoples never to go to war with one another again. We are resolved that the method of consultation shall be the method adopted to deal with any other questions that may concern our two countries.

As he read on it became apparent that the Munich Agreement, as it was being called, was popular with the press and the public, who perceived it as having prevented a war with Germany. The editorial in the *Daily Express* pretty well summed up how everybody seemed to feel. He read:

Be glad in your hearts. Give thanks to God. People of Britain your children are safe. Your husbands and sons will not march to war. Peace is a victory for all mankind.

If we must have a victor, let us choose Chamberlain. For the Prime Minister's conquests are mighty and enduring — millions of happy homes and hearts relieved of their burden. To him the laurels.

And now let us go back to our own affairs. We have had enough of these menaces, conjured up from the Continent to confuse us.

Biff bit his lip. It seemed a great relief, but he only hoped that they would continue to build up the strength of the Air Force from the perilously low state to which it had been allowed to slump.

For heaven's sake, the Navy still seemed strong enough.

Apart from Anthony Eden resigning earlier in the year as foreign secretary in protest at the policy of appeasement, on the day, only Winston Churchill raised a dissenting voice.

Whatever, it was a lovely start to their honeymoon.

He turned the page. Inside were splendid photographs of the launching of the new liner, the *Queen Elizabeth*, at Clydebank.

On the sports page was an article on Don Budge who had become the first tennis player to achieve the Gland Slam. After that he dozed for a while. The last few days — and one night, had been quite draining.

The Channel was calm, and Biff stood on the stern of the steamer with his arm around Rosemary's waist as they watched the white cliffs recede. She turned her face to his.

When he kissed her he could taste the salt on her lips.

That night they dined in the Ritz's ornate restaurant, and drank wine the like of which he had never tasted before. He felt a bit guilty because his father-in-law was paying: it had been set up beforehand as part of their wedding gift.

Maybe it was because they were tired from travelling, or were suffering from the excess of wine and food, but they didn't make love that night. Nothing was said or decided. They just fell into bed and went straight to sleep.

In the morning there wasn't time for such dalliances, as they overslept and had to be awakened in a hurry in order to get the Rome express. He managed to get that very day's *Manchester Guardian*, of all things, from a new arrival at the Ritz, who'd flown to Paris that morning. They jumped into the taxi the doorman was holding for them.

On the way through the Paris streets he noticed that the news-stands carried more *München* announcements, only this time the name Daladier featured more prominently.

Settled on the train, so excitingly and distinctively foreign from the ones at home, Rosemary was absolutely in her seventh heaven.

'Oh, I'm so glad we came, aren't you darling? Fancy being stuck in the cottage in the Gloucestershire rain.'

He chuckled. 'Oh, I don't know. We could

have had more fun this morning if we had been.'

She gave him a stern look, but her eyes were twinkling. 'I haven't married a monster, have I?'

He grinned. 'We shall have to see.'

As they rolled through the flat lands and wide fields south of Paris he began to read the paper.

No stranger experience can have happened to Mr Chamberlain during the past month of adventures than his reception back home in London. He drove from Heston to Buckingham Palace, where the crowd clamoured for him, and within five minutes of his arrival he was standing on the balcony of the Palace with the King and Queen and Mrs Chamberlain.

The cries were all for 'Neville', and he stood there blinking in the light of a powerful arc lamp and waving his hand and smiling. For three minutes this demonstration lasted.

Another welcome awaited the Premier in Downing Street, which he reached fifteen minutes later. With difficulty his car moved forward from Whitehall to No. 10. Mounted police rode fore and aft and a constable kept guard on the running board of the car.

He looked up, watched the steam drifting away across the fields as they picked up speed. It had obviously been a dreadful worry to many people, more than his young generation had realized. He read on:

Everywhere people were cheering. One of the women found no other words to express her feelings but these. 'The man who gave me back my son.'

Mr and Mrs Chamberlain stood for a few moments on the doorstep acknowledging the greeting. Then Mr Chamberlain went to a first-floor window and leaned forward, happily smiling on the people. 'My good friends,' he said — it took some time to still the clamour so that he might be heard. 'This is the second time in our history that there has come back from Germany 'peace with honour'. I believe it is peace for our time.'

It was all very encouraging. As he lowered the paper his eyes found Rosemary. She looked radiant, and happy. At least she would have the honeymoon she had dreamed of. That, at least, for the moment, was something to be thankful for.

4

Everybody seemed to be laughing. Biff suddenly realized that it was evoked by the senior judge, making his speech at the luncheon. He'd just told an anecdote where the ceremonial splendour of judges and high sheriff in procession at an opening of the law year somewhere, had taken the wrong turning, and filed in solemn, glorious order through a working court, and out through another door, much to the sitting judge's amazement, to say nothing of that of the terrified defendant.

The speech ended with a toast to the high sheriff. Biff tried to get to his feet, but they were all too quick for him. The woman put her hand reassuringly on his shoulder and gently restrained him. 'It's all right. They don't expect it.' She meant well, but it left him feeling sad and old; old and lonely. He looked around the room. Apart from Jimmy on the next table there was nobody left from his generation. He shook his head sadly and reached for his glass of wine. *Nobody.*

He didn't count those lost during the war of course — how could you, *that* was different — and unforgettable — but afterwards, when they had been starting out afresh. To begin with you lost the odd friend — illness or accident when you were in your forties. Nothing happened then for twenty years, until slowly the Grim Reaper started his work, and at last it dawned on you that there were an awful lot of faces suddenly not around any more. Then death began to get closer, personal, until finally . . . even now he got he got a lump in his throat. Maybe it was his age: he was an old man who couldn't control his emotions.

'Dad — you all right?'

It was his daughter, who had quietly come across the room, looking concerned.

'Yes, dear — just thinking of your mother.'

He patted her hand as it rested on his shoulder.

The high sheriff moved to the microphone, shuffled his notes. 'Your Grace, my lords, ladies and gentlemen.'

His daughter scuttled back to her seat.

He remembered his own speech, back in 1988, with his wife watching him from the other side of the table. He'd spoken of tradition, of men who should have been there, who had been denied their life, denied the chance to have children, to see them grow up, go through school, university, marriage and have grandchildren. And the tragedy was on the other, enemy, side as well — whatever the circumstances, whoever was to blame. He had glanced across at his wife who nodded, as if to say thank you for not forgetting.

* * *

The taxi picked its way through the bustling streets of Sorrento, the driver honking his horn, gesticulating and shouting at anyone holding up his progress.

Rosemary clung to his arm.

'My God — does he think this is a race or something?'

Biff grinned. 'I can see why they love their Grands Prix.'

His gaze went back to his window. Little restaurants and cafés were everywhere, occupying any part of the pavement that was allowed.

Little old women dressed in black haggled as they felt and tested the fruit and vegetables beneath the picturesque and peeling walls of old sun-drenched town houses and apartments. And everywhere there were churches.

Horses, carts, and motor cars clogged the narrow streets, but every now and then the shimmering blue water of the Bay of Naples showed between the buildings.

He noticed the gardens, growing all sorts of vegetables, and with vines curling around little trellised terraces. Obviously the heart of every Italian town-dweller still belonged in the country.

And then he saw a group of stern-looking men on the corner of a junction. *Il Duce*'s men in their black shirts and ties, silver collar patches and grey-green trousers, topped by black fezzes with tassels. Somehow it didn't seem to chime with the sunny disposition of the Italians. Still, he had to admit the trains were spotless and ran on time, just as everybody had said, and the streets were very clean. From their carriage window they'd seen a huge straight road near Naples which had been built by Mussolini for the ever growing number of cars. He'd heard about *autobahns*, as they were called in Germany. Some said there was a military purpose behind them.

Eventually they reached a wider square from which roads led in all directions. Here were larger restaurants with outdoor tables, partly under cover, as in Paris, with shady Roman pine trees in abundance. It was the centre of Sorrento, the Piazza Tasse. The taxi swung through a gateway flanked by large stone columns and open wrought-iron gates. Biff just caught a glimpse of a sign bearing the name of the hotel in gold-coloured lettering. He squeezed her hand. 'Here we are, darling.'

The long, straight driveway led them through five acres of golden orange groves and bright flowers before opening into a wide turning circle dominated by pine trees, and, framed by the deep-blue sea behind it, a magnificent nineteenth-century building, its large windows adorned with green louvred shutters.

The car drew to a halt before the main entrance. Immediately a uniformed commissionaire came down the steps and opened Biff's door as a porter in a similarly coloured jacket made a beeline for the back of the vehicle with his barrow.

Biff stepped out and was greeted with a salute and a '*Buon giorno, signore.*'

He nodded and smiled as he turned and held out his hand to help Rosemary as she slid across the leather of the back seat.

She stood up, blinking in the strong sunlight, and gazed at the façade of the hotel.

'Biff, it's just beautiful.'

He paid the driver and started up the steps with her.

'This is where Enrico Caruso stayed in 1921.'

'Did Queen Victoria come — is that why it's called Victoria?'

He shrugged. 'No idea, but we can ask. Certainly the British have been staying here for years. Edward VII came in 1910.'

They entered a cool hallway with a floor of blue and white marble squares which now had a worn, aged look that added to the feeling of elegance. Two huge porcelain jars flanked the reception desk. To the left a grand staircase led up to a landing where a large statue from classical antiquity stood in an alcove, the cream walls decorated with frescoes of heraldic and Grecian designs.

They reached the reception desk, made of dark mahogany. A man in a black coat and stripped trousers came forward to greet them.

'Mr and Mrs Banks? My name is Georgio Catino. I am the manager and may I personally welcome you to the Victoria.'

Biff took the proffered hand, followed by Rosemary, who said: 'Thank you. It's beautiful.'

'Thank you, *signora*. I hope you had a good journey?'

Biff nodded. 'Yes. Your trains are excellent.'

Catino beckoned a clerk forward to attend to them.

It was then that Biff noticed another man at the back of the reception area in a dark suit. He seemed to be paying them an inordinate amount of attention — actually staring at them.

Catino noticed that Biff was frowning and said quickly: 'We shall need to keep your passports for a day or so, and you need to fill in these rather large forms, I'm afraid. Modern travel is so much more complicated than it used to be, is it not?'

He said it apologetically.

Biff handed over their stiff-covered dark-blue passports.

The clerk took them and turned away as Biff started to fill in the rather detailed form, which he found irritating. The manager realized this and fussed around, trying to help.

Biff looked up to ask Rosemary something and noticed that the man in the dark suit was already studying their passports, looking up occasionally in their direction, then resuming his study. Biff realized he must be with immigration or the frontier police, or something official.

He glowered. 'Is everything all right?'

The man eyed him before replying: 'I see you are a pilot, Mr Banks.'

'Yes, that's correct.'

'What do you fly?'

'Aeroplanes.' Biff didn't try to hide the sarcasm in his voice, but he wondered if they were going to get on to the fact that he was in the Royal Air Force — a *military* pilot.

Suddenly the man snapped the passport

shut and unexpectedly grinned.

'You are on your honeymoon, I believe?'

Frowning, Biff said: 'Yes. How did you know that?'

Still smiling, but retaining the passports, the man nodded at Rosemary.

'Such a beautiful young lady. Obviously much in love. I hope you have a wonderful time in our country. I think you will be impressed by what you see. *Il Duce* has made great changes.'

With that he gave a little bow, turned on his heel and went through a door in the back.

Catino was visibly relieved.

Biff asked, 'Who was that?'

The manager looked uncomfortable. 'Signore Franchetti of the *Milizia di Frontiera* — one of *Il Duce*'s men.'

Biff nodded. 'I see. A major, no less.'

He knew the rank structure of the Blackshirts from a RAF briefing.

Catino gestured with his hands towards the staircase.

'Yes, yes. Now, let me show you to your room.' His face beamed. 'If you have no objection we would like to offer you one of our top suites — at no extra charge,' he added hurriedly.

Biff was genuinely surprised.

'Why, that's awfully decent of you. Is there any reason?'

'Because you are honeymooners, and besides, we don't have as many visitors as we used to, so we have the room. Please, it will be my pleasure.'

Impatient with Biff, Rosemary butted in.

'Why, thank you, Mr Catino. We are pleased to accept.'

They followed the manager as he escorted them up the stairs and put the key in to one of a pair of double doors.

'Here we are.'

He opened the door and stood aside for them. Rosemary went first, and Biff almost bumped into her because she had stopped so abruptly.

The room was large, with a painted ceiling depicting gods and goddesses being borne by chariots over fluffy clouds. The walls were covered in silk of a faint gold hue. Between two french windows draped in matching silk curtains was a white marble fireplace.

Assorted sofas and chairs were placed around it, while a delicate writing bureau and chair were placed against the opposite wall. The marble floor was covered with two huge Persian rugs.

'Good heavens.' Rosemary found her voice. 'It's beautiful.'

Catino beamed, and opened another double door.

'And this is your bedroom.'

They followed him into another room, this time with no frescoes. The vast bed was set against one pale blue wall, which showed off the elaborate headboard. There was another marble fireplace, and a table and chairs in the style of Louis XVI, and rugs filled the room, with huge wardrobes and chests of drawers spaced around the walls.

'Here is the bathroom.'

Catino opened a concealed door and flicked on a light-switch.

The honey-coloured marble was laid from floor to ceiling. Lights were reflected in the large mirrors above the two art deco basins.

Rosemary just looked in, then said; 'It's sumptuous.'

'I hope you will enjoy your stay with us. If there is anything we can do to make you more comfortable, please don't hesitate to ask.'

Their luggage arrived. Two porters placed their cases on a table, Rosemary's hatbox on the bed, and trunk in the corner.

'Would you like a maid to unpack for you?'

Rosemary chuckled. 'No, that's quite all right thank you. I like doing it myself.'

'Of course.'

After further pleasantries Catino withdrew. They looked at each other for a second, then

Biff picked Rosemary up and swung her around as they laughed, then kissed.

He said: 'It's wonderful, darling. We'll remember this for the rest of our lives.'

She agreed. 'But why do you think they've done this?'

He made for one of the french doors.

'I expect it's because fewer people are travelling with all this talk of war.'

He threw open the doors and stepped out on to a large terrace, the stone balustrade marked at each end by a Roman bust.

'Come and look at this.'

The view was spectacular. The hotel was on a cliff edge so they were looking down on to the harbour some two to three hundred feet below, where a paddle steamer churned the water as it manoeuvred to head out to sea to Capri. Along to their right the cliff edge of Sorrento was solid with old hotels and buildings built right to the edge.

Opposite, across the Bay of Naples loomed Europe's only mainland volcano: Mount Vesuvius, looking quiescent in the haze.

Hundreds of little sailing boats plied out of the harbour. The steamer sounded its siren several times, and began to make headway, leaving a white wake of foam in the deep blue which turned to clear sparkling green in the shadows. He put his arm around her as she came and stood beside him.

'Isn't that just marvellous?' She placed her arm around him.

'Darling, you can see why I wanted to come here now?'

He gave her a squeeze as she added: 'Thanks for putting up with the journey.'

He smiled and kissed the side of her head. 'I've always been fascinated by ancient Rome. We can visit Pompeii from here. You know about Pompeii, don't you?'

She scolded him.

'Do you think we girls don't get the same lessons as you boys? Do you think we get just cookery and Jane Austen?'

'Sorry.'

She took his hand and led him back into the coolness of the room. There was no question about what she intended as she sat on the bed and kicked off her shoes.

'Well, husband, to your duty.'

Biff still couldn't get over her lack of shyness. Even on their second attempt at being married he had been fumbling all over the place until Rosemary had taken positive action and guided him into her — digging her nails into his back as she winced, just the once.

It was only now that he was beginning to realize that an educated, horse-loving woman of the thirties was not like the girls he had dreamed about.

So he ran his hand boldly up her leg and under her skirt to the top of her stocking, and on over her smooth skin and suspender.

Rosemary suddenly reached up and pulled him down on to her.

Clothes went in all directions and he barely made it before he was fusing with her body in a violent, energetic thrusting that had her hanging on to him with her legs as if she was out with the hounds.

When at last he rolled off her she was up in a flash, kissing him and ruffling his hair, and giggling like a schoolgirl as she slipped out of the rest of her clothes, trailing them on the floor, and disappeared into the bathroom.

He heard the shower running as she hummed a tune.

Biff Banks felt as if *he'd* been biffed.

He lay looking up at the ceiling, at the pattern of light dappling the cornices. What a wonderful thing marriage was, and how lucky he was. Rosemary was beautiful, talented and incredibly sensuous. What more could a man ask for? The sound of the shower ceased.

She came back into the room with only a white towel wrapped around her, shaking her hair free from the cap she had been wearing.

'God, that was terrific. It's so hot.'

With that she went out on to the terrace. Biff, dressed only in his striped dressing-gown, took his cigarettes out to the table. Rosemary was leaning over the balustrade looking out across the bay.

He frowned. 'Darling — you're not dressed,' he warned.

She turned. Laughed.

'You're such a fuddy duddy.'

With that she let the towel fall, and popped into the chair beside him, took one of his cigarettes and crossed her legs.

'Light me up, please, darling.'

Biff's jaw dropped.

'My God, woman.'

He looked wildly around, but realized with relief that where they were, it would be difficult for her to be seen. He looked back at her again, at her small breasts dazzling in the bright light, at the golden freckles that wound down her arms and legs and at her painted toes. It was both erotic and surreal, as if one of the ornamental figures had come alive. She giggled and prompted:

'The light, darling?'

He flicked open his lighter top and at the second attempt applied the flame to the end of the cigarette. She took a long pull, sat back and breathed out smoke, making rings.

He shook his head in disbelief.

'Where, oh where, did you learn to do that?'

She put her other arm across her chest to hold the elbow of the arm with the cigarette, pushing up her breasts.

'Where else? School.'

He shook his head.

'What am I going to do with you?'

He knew as soon as he said it that was a mistake.

She looked back at him from under her half-closed, long eyelashes.

'I hope you'll think of something.'

So he did. But she had to wait until that night.

★ ★ ★

Everybody seemed to be looking at him.

Then he realized that the high sheriff had said something about him, and they had all turned — clapping. He had not the slightest idea what had been said, but he got an inkling of what it might have been when the woman, still clapping, said in his ear,

'Did the Queen put it on you herself?'

She obviously meant the DFC he'd won in 1942. The fact that she thought the Queen had been the monarch then, he was quite resigned to. The appalling lack of knowledge about the history of their country and its geography, he had got used to many years ago. God only knew what they taught in schools these days.

He just said 'Yes,' and dipped his head in acknowledgement to the high sheriff.

The speech continued, was all about the wonderful people in the county — far more than the present incumbent had ever realized — who volunteered to do unpaid work in the community to help people of all ages, in health and sickness, to make their lives better. It was his opinion that the county would be a far poorer place without them.

There was an enthusiastic response from the audience, and Biff receded thankfully into the background again. He didn't like any allusion to the medal. He knew so many men more worthy, who had never made it to Buck House, or to the end for that matter, to see the final victory. Their resting places were unknown: they had died so that the nice young woman to his left could be so ignorant of the history of the country, if the country so wished.

Biff couldn't help wonder whether without their sacrifice, she might have been better educated — in German history.

German history . . .

5

They'd been there for two days, doing nothing in particular, just taking the sun on the hotel's pontoons at the foot of the cliff, swimming in the clear blue-green water, looking at the seabed with its colourful fish and plants, and generally resting after their journey.

On the third day they decided to go to Pompeii, to the Roman ruins and the continuing excavations.

The hotel had arranged taxis as several people were going.

When they gathered in the entrance hall there was a gentleman wearing an old-fashioned canvas jacket and waistcoat with spats on his shoes, striped trousers, and sporting a monocle, and several elderly ladies without escorts — widows of the Great War no doubt. About eight other people — couples — were there also, some they had seen around the hotel, had even become on nodding terms with at breakfast.

One couple was standing to one side.

Rosemary smiled at the woman who smiled back. Biff didn't really want to join up with anybody, especially as they looked English. The man was wearing a double-breasted dark-blue blazer, with short, high lapels, and six brass buttons down the front, done up.

His cravat was in a dark maroon that complimented his rather racy pink shirt. Grey flannels completed his kit.

Biff felt a little scruffy. Because of the possibility of its being a hot day he wore his blue shirt with its wide collar outside his rather crumpled summer jacket, and with his white cricket bags as trousers.

The girl, though, he had to admit, was a stunner, dressed in a light summer frock, rather like Rosemary's, but it seemed to be in a very *risqué* material: he fancied he caught sight of the outline of her legs when she stepped into a ray of sunlight.

He pulled Rosemary gently away towards the reception desk.

'I need to ask about the passports.'

She was puzzled.

'Why? They'll give them back when they're ready.'

'You don't want to get involved, do you?' he hissed. 'They could be as boring as hell. He looks like some flash chap from the City who wants to tell us how much he earned last year.'

Rosemary shook her head.

'No, she looks really nice to me — and he is obviously an outdoor type. You're just being miserable.'

He knew she was right.

The man in the old-fashioned kit suddenly clapped his hands and called out:

'Is everybody here for the Pompeii excursion? Please put your hand up if you are.'

Rosemary, holding her arm in the air looked around. All seemed to be going, including the young, good-looking blond fellow with the dark-haired girl who appeared to be such a 'sport'.

The elderly man continued:

'Do you mind if I speak mostly in English? Everybody seems to be able to understand, and it will save me saying things over and over again. Of course, if anybody needs clarification on any point, I do speak French, German and . . . ' he shrugged and rolled his eyes, 'Italian.' The ladies laughed at his joke.

'Now, the taxis are waiting outside. Let us all get aboard — yes!'

Everyone milled around the door and then walked to the cars lined up in the drive. Biff and Rosemary made for the one furthest away.

Settled into the back, they waited to see whom they would be sharing with, but everybody seemed to find room elsewhere, and in the end they set off with just the two of them on the hour-long journey.

The sight of the city frozen in time by the eruption of Vesuvius was nothing short of breathtaking.

As the group moved from one building to the next in the huge excavation, they listened in rapture to their guide.

Rosemary was particularly taken with the house of the Vettii, especially the fresco in the entrance of Priapus, weighing his manliness on scales against a bag of gold and, in another room, a sculpture of the same god, with a huge phallus that had once been a fountain.

The elderly ladies seemed to be whispering a lot, and Rosemary and the other young English woman, though not standing together, seemed to be communicating across the group by half-suppressed giggles and glances.

Biff felt acutely embarrassed; it would never have been allowed at home.

Luncheon was laid out at a nearby restaurant. As Biff and Rosemary shuffled into the dining-room with its view down to the sea, they found that they were going to be sharing a table with the other young couple.

For a second they all hesitated, then Rosemary held out her hand to the woman.

'I'm Rosemary.'

The woman took it, and said in beautiful English:

'And I'm Anna.'

She was the same height as Rosemary, but she had dark wavy hair, with lighter threads running through, falling in soft waves to her neck and curling over her forehead. Her face was symmetrical, her nose small; her dark-brown eyes, surrounded by long lashes, were bright with intelligence and humour and under eyebrows that had been only gently plucked. Her mouth was generous and full with just a hint of lipstick.

'This is my husband.'

The man was a couple of inches taller than Biff, but slimmer. His face, topped by a shock of blond hair brushed straight back with a parting on one side, was narrower but healthy-looking — like that of somebody who was always out of doors; it was a very patrician-looking face. He had a firm jaw with a dimple, and a strong nose, and his eyebrows and lashes were darker than his hair. His eyes were an intense pale blue. He gave a very slight bow and the faintest of a click of the heels.

'Good morning, my name is Julius von Riegner,' he grinned, 'but they call me Konrad after my grandfather.' He held out his hand.

Biff was flabbergasted. They were *Germans*. His mouth wouldn't work for a moment, then he managed a strained: 'How do you do.'

He reluctantly took the offered hand, and shook it — just the once, saying: 'And I'm Jack Banks, but they call me Biff. Rosemary is my wife.'

Von Riegner lifted the back of Rosemary's hand to his mouth, and touched it, briefly with his lips, but Biff settled for shaking Anna's hand, finding it long and elegant. The diamond ring was substantial and spoke of great wealth.

'Biff?' The German inclined his head. 'What does that mean? I haven't heard the name before.'

He spoke with only a very slight accent, had obviously, like his wife, had an expensive education.

Biff shrugged, and mimed an upper cut, despite the man's obvious command of the language.

'It's from my boxing days.'

Although Konrad had obviously understood, Anna spoke in German, explaining.

Her husband looked at her and said something back, then turned to Biff and Rosemary:

'Pardon us, my wife is a — how do you say

it — a linguist, and she also makes it her job to make sure I've fully understood. She needs to be in control you see,' he added with a mischievous grin. She hit him playfully on the arm and said to them in perfect English:

'I'm sorry, but my new husband is still trying to be the boss — he really should know better and leave that sort of thing behind on his boat.'

Her accent was flawless.

Rosemary giggled. 'I'm having problems too, with mine.' This was news to Biff. 'Have you been married long?'

Anna rolled her eyes.

'On our honeymoon, no less.'

Chuckling Rosemary answered: 'I thought so; we are too.'

'Really.'

The girls had obviously taken an instant liking to each other. Rosemary's blonde hair, pulled back that morning in a ponytail ready for the day's activities, bobbed up and down as she rattled on to Anna; the two women were soon in a conversation about their weddings as they sat down at the table. The men followed suit, and studied the menus.

Because they were obviously getting on so well, and Konrad seemed a decent enough fellow despite being German, Biff tried to think of something to say to break the silence between them. Manners demanded it.

'Boat? You are a sailor, then?'

Konrad looked guarded momentarily, but then said: 'Yes, but not on the sea at the moment.'

'Oh.' Biff didn't know what to make of that. Perhaps they had to wait for cargoes to come along or something; he knew nothing of the operations of the mercantile marine.

'And you Biff, what do you do?'

For a fleeting second Biff wondered whether he should reveal that he was a pilot, Konrad being German, then he thought; hang it, he wasn't giving away a state secret.

'I'm in the Royal Air Force: a pilot.'

Konrad's eyes widened. For a moment he looked stunned, then he chuckled apologetically. Biff frowned.

'What's funny?'

'I have not been as honest with you as you have with me. Please forgive me. I'm an officer in the *Kriegsmarine* — our navy, although at the moment I have a shore appointment, looking after a dotty old admiral.'

They both paused, taking in the fact that they were in the same business, defenders of their countries, in a time of international uncertainty.

Biff realized that Konrad was as uncomfortable as he was; it had been so unexpected.

He couldn't help but smile.

'And we are both on honeymoon. What else do we have in common?'

Konrad nodded at the girls. 'They are both beautiful, and we are handsome — are we not?'

He threw his arms wide.

Laughing, Biff agreed.

'Are you enjoying Italy?'

It was Anna, looking directly at him with those incredible eyes.

'Of course; it's very beautiful, and the people are so friendly.'

She nodded. 'I've always wanted to come here,' she shot a mischievous glance at Konrad, 'but my husband wanted to go to boring old Switzerland — *again*.'

Konrad protested. 'Come now, my dear, you've always enjoyed Lucerne and Geneva.'

Those beautiful eyes flashed. 'Yes, that's exactly it. I wanted to go somewhere completely different for my honeymoon, and I've heard so much about Naples, and Sorrento and the Amalfi coast.'

Rosemary broke in enthusiastically.

'Me too. It's such a romantic place.'

Anna agreed. 'When you look out on that bay,' she waved at the window, 'and see Vesuvius, it's amazing to think that the Romans saw exactly the same scene as they went about their daily business.'

Rosemary nodded vigorously, her ponytail shaking about her neck.

The girls started off again.

Biff shook his head. 'You both speak excellent English.'

Konrad smiled. 'Thank you. It was required at my academy; you couldn't get out of it even if you wanted to — and I didn't. I've always admired the English. After all, you are fellow Saxons, are you not?'

Biff could see that Konrad was having a little go at him, in good fun.

'Yes, but not Prussians, thank God. Where are you from?'

Konrad winced.

'*Touché*. I'm from Erlangen — it's in Bavaria, but my wife is from Berlin. That's where I met her. She's not really German, though; she can trace her ancestry back to the Huguenots.' He gave her a gentle prod in the side. 'You're really French, aren't you, my love?'

Anna stopped talking for a second at this interruption, to look at him in mock disdain.

'Your family are all peasants — despite the *von*!'

He roared with laughter.

They were interrupted by the waiter, who took their orders, then enquired about what to drink?

Local wine was a natural choice, and mineral water — 'senza gaz.' Biff struggled with his few words, but Anna rattled something off in Italian and the waiter replied. In a rare slip in her command of English she nodded.

'Ja, that will be fine.'

Because they had only heard her speak in perfect English up to then, the 'Ja' came as a shock, and reminded Biff at least, to be careful what he said. They were so normal — just like themselves. Could they be carefully planted spies?

Then he asked himself with embarrassment who did he think he was? Someone bearing high military secrets that the German Government had sent their top team to intercept?

He must have been grinning because Konrad said: 'Penny for them?'

Startled, Biff flustered. 'Oh, sorry, I was thinking of something that happened at a restaurant back home. Please, how rude of me. Now, what are you planning for the rest of your stay? When do you go back to Germany?'

Konrad waved his hand elegantly in the air.

'We have plans to go to Capri — of course — and then a drive up the coast. Mostly we play tennis, drink and enjoy the sun. It's going to get cold when we return to Germany.'

The thought of autumn didn't worry Biff. 'I like the colours of the trees. It's a beautiful time of the year.'

Anna leaned across.

'A time of mists and mellow fruitfulness.'

Rosemary was astounded. 'You know Keats?'

'Of course. I have a degree from Heidelberg University in English studies, which includes literature.'

Konrad drawled: 'That's all very well, Biff old sport, but it's going to get bloody cold. Winter's coming, is it not?'

Anna winced at the put-on frightful stage accent of her husband.

'Oh God, Konrad, shut up, you fool, you sound like a character from a Noël Coward play.'

'Oh.' He appealed to Biff for support. 'You see what I've married? She is an ogress.'

He got a thump for his troubles.

Maybe it was the wine, but as the meal progressed they got more and more noisy and animated, talking of sport, art, music — anything but current affairs.

When eventually the time came to board the fleet of taxis back to the hotel, they made sure they were in the same one: Biff in the front, with Konrad in the back, a girl on either side.

Somebody started singing 'O Sole Mio'. After they had murdered it, at least as might be judged from the look in the taxi driver's eyes, Anna started up with 'It's a long way to Tipperary, It's a long way to go . . .'

For a moment Biff was stunned, but Konrad, breaking off from joining in with the girls explained: 'We all know this song from the Tommies in the war. It's very good.'

So Biff sang as well. When they had finished Konrad all on his own started singing softly, a haunting refrain.

Vor der Kaserne bei dem großen Tor
Stand eine Lanterne and steht sie noch davor
So wollen wir uns wieder seh'n
Bei der Lanterne wollen wir steh'n
Wie einst Lile Marlen.

Anna winced. 'It's new, he's been practising it at home on the piano. He was lucky to get the sheet music, Goebbels doesn't like it. I wouldn't mind so much but he sings along as well, it's driving me insane.'

He grinned mischievously at her. 'It's a lovely tune, very sad and romantic.'

By the time they had got back to the hotel

they were all half-asleep from the food, wine and warmth. In the hotel lobby they faced each other.

Anna said 'I'm going to take a shower and have a sleep.'

Rosemary agreed. 'Good idea.'

On impulse the girls leant forward and kissed each other on the cheek.

'Might see you later, at dinner?'

Anna looked hopeful. Rosemary nodded, smiling.

'That would be fine. Meet in the bar at say . . . eight o'clock?'

'Excellent.'

Biff and Konrad exchanged glances of mock resignation as the German said: 'see what I mean, Biff? We are not bosses in our own lives any more.'

'Come along, Oberleutnant zur See.'

Anna took him by the arm and started pulling him away, waving with her fingers only to Biff. 'See you later then.'

When they'd gone Rosemary said: 'They really are very nice, aren't they? You were completely wrong about them.'

He acknowledged her remark with a nod as he took her hand and made for their staircase.

'I know, I know. But I thought they were English, and not quite right. How was I to know they were Germans?'

'Can't tell the difference really, can you?' Rosemary taunted as he put the key in the door and opened it.

On a sudden impulse he picked her up. Rosemary gave a little squeak of surprise as he flipped the door shut behind them with his heel.

'Right, young lady, just so as you know who is boss.'

He dumped her on the bed, and flung his jacket off as she lay still, looking up at him.

'Oh, you're so masterful.'

Even he realized it must have been the wine talking.

6

They were first down, and ordered two dry martinis. When the von Riegners eventually showed up Anna looked radiant. 'Sorry we're late.'

Rosemary and she exchanged knowing suggestive glances as Biff ordered two more drinks.

Before dinner they talked of families. Anna's parents lived in Berlin, her father was a professor at the university, in the department of medicine, Konrad's parents were more elderly, and had moved to Bamberg, a larger town than Erlangen.

'They have found a much better apartment, close to shops and the bank. It is much more convenient for them.'

'What does your father do?' asked Biff.

Konrad had taken out a packet of cigars and offered them. Biff had declined, but Konrad had begun lighting one. When he finished he screwed his eyes up in the cloud of blue smoke as he disposed of his match into a tray. He took the cigar out of his mouth.

'Nothing any more. He is . . . ' he paused

and questioned Anna in German who replied in English: 'Retired.'

'Yes, retired — he is retired now,' continued Konrad, 'but he was a naval man also.'

He looked sheepish and added: 'He fought at the Skagerrakschlacht.'

Frowning, Biff was just going to say he hadn't heard of it when Anna broke off what she was saying to Rosemary to interject: 'You call it the Battle of Jutland.'

Konrad added: 'He was injured; his ship sank, you see.'

Since it was obviously the Royal Navy that had sent it to the bottom Biff, out of good manners managed: 'I'm sorry to hear that.'

'Don't be; he did rather well out of it. Won the Iron Cross and survived the rest of the war.'

Biff felt a little uncomfortable talking about the war, but Konrad seemed quite happy. 'And your father?'

Biff nodded. 'Infantry Officer. Stopped a Blighty one at Gallipoli.'

Konrad was about to draw on his cigar again but paused. 'Stopped a Blighty one?'

Before Anna could intervene Biff said quickly: 'He was wounded, severely enough to have to go back to England.'

'Ah.' Realization dawned.

Konrad continued to draw on his cigar before saying: 'We are both lucky, then. Our fathers came through.'

They lapsed into silence, sipping their martinis, conscious that both families knew about service — and suffering.

The atmosphere over dinner was lively. They discussed the latest shows; Konrad and Anna had both been to New York on the Hamburg Line.

'The skyline was fantastic when we approached in the morning,' said Anna. 'The skyscrapers come out of the mist.'

They'd been up the Empire State Building. 'No sign of gorillas,' joked Konrad in reference to the *King Kong* film.

Anna had enjoyed the shows on Broadway, especially *Babes in Arms* and a song from it: 'The Lady is a Tramp' and her husband had visited the Stock Exchange.

'Like a madhouse, Biff — a bloody madhouse. I don't understand Americans; no class, it's all money, money, money.'

Diplomatically, Biff made no comment, although privately he was thinking of Anna's ring and the obvious old wealth of Konrad's family.

They took coffee and brandies in the art nouveau garden room. The white grand piano was being played by a Negro, his teeth gleaming against the dark of his face and dinner jacket, smiling as he crooned a love song.

'He's just like Hutch,' said Rosemary dreamily.

Whether it was the food, the warmth, or the excesses of the day, everybody seemed sleepy, and by 11.30 they had finished drinking and talking. They started to get up to go to bed, walking slowly along the length of the room.

'What are you doing tomorrow?' asked Rosemary.

Anna glanced at Konrad before saying: 'We have nothing planned. Just going to stay around, play some tennis, take the sun.'

Rosemary stopped. 'Tennis. You can play tennis?'

Anna looked puzzled. 'Of course.'

'What about us having our own tennis party — mixed doubles, or men against the women and maybe singles?' Rosemary was quite excited.

Anna too was enthusiastic.

'That would be good.'

Without further ado the girls set a time.

'We'd better book the court now. First session in your name, second in ours. That should be enough, don't you think?' Anna put her head to one side.

As she and Rosemary made towards the front desk, Biff and Konrad looked at each other.

'Well, it seems our day is already decided for us.' Konrad smiled. 'Do you like tennis?'

Biff grinned. 'If I'm playing with Anna and Rosemary, yes.'

Konrad slapped him on the back.

'That's true. I'll see you in the morning then, at whatever time these wives of ours have decided.'

With that he started up the stairs.

'Tell Anna not to wake me up,' he called over his shoulder, winking.

★ ★ ★

The best tactical player was Rosemary. Anna was more athletic. Biff and Konrad were aggressive; stronger, but essentially wilder. Rosemary and Biff just got their nose ahead in the final match.

They crashed into the chairs beside the court.

Biff caught the attention of a waiter, who came over to them from the striped refreshment tent that the hotel had set up on the lawn for the season.

'May we have a big bottle of water; *senza gaz*, and cordials for everybody?'

Konrad waved his arm. 'I would also like a large glass of beer please, and . . . ' He added something in German.

The waiter chuckled, shot a glance at Biff as he went off.

'What did you say to him?' asked Rosemary.

Konrad grinned and looked slyly at Biff.

'I only said to make sure the beer was cold, not like my English friend would like it.'

Immediately Biff sat upright, snorting.

'What utter rubbish. All the light stuff you drink has to be cold — it's tasteless. We brew real beer.'

'*Ja — warm* beer.'

Konrad was grinning from ear to ear.

Biff shook his head.

'It's not warm, it's room temperature, the way it's supposed to be drunk so that you can get the full flavour of the hops. You don't chill red wine, do you?'

Shaking his head Konrad held up his hands in mock surrender.

'You win, you win.'

They lapsed into comfortable silence.

The waiter returned, effortlessly carrying a very large tray in one hand, and without setting it down, dispensed four cordials, then the water, and placing, last of all, a very large glass of beer in front of Konrad.

Rosemary exclaimed: 'Gosh, are you going to drink all of that?'

Konrad pulled himself upright and reached for the glass.

'Very easily, my dear.'

They watched as he started drinking, the level of beer slowly going down until the by now horizontal glass showed empty, just foam sliding down its side as he set it back on to the table.

'*Konrad*!'

Anna shook her head and said to them. 'He still plays these silly drinking games they have in the Navy.'

Her husband wiped the back of his hand across his mouth.

'No, no, we don't do things like that.'

He winked at Biff. 'I learned that at my daddy's knee in Munich, at the *Oktoberfest*.'

Anna shook her head.

'He may have, but believe me, I've seen him next day after some dinner or other in the mess and I *know* he's been up to no good.'

Konrad looked at Biff for support.

'Come now, Biff,' he implored, 'tell my bossy wife that you have celebration nights in your Air Force.'

Biff hadn't really had much experience with such things yet, but he knew of their wild reputation, especially after the brass had withdrawn. Mark you, they had had their moments in the training squadron.

He smiled at Anna.

'Of course, we all do it, makes for *esprit de corps*.'

Konrad took out a cigar from his tennis bag and offered it to Biff who shook his head. 'There you are, Anna,' exclaimed Konrad. 'Good for you, Biff.'

Anna looked to Rosemary for support.

Rolling their eyes they raised their glasses to each other in mutual agreement at the childishness of men.

After they had sat talking, and had long finished their drinks, Rosemary stood up, smoothing down her white skirt.

'Right, I'm off for a shower and a lie-down. You coming, Biff?'

As he rose they all did, and made their way back to the hotel, rackets over shoulders.

Rosemary led the way up the stairs. 'See you in the bar at seven, then? Whoever is first gets the champagne going.'

Inside their rooms Rosemary propped the tennis racket in its wooden press near the door. She went to the dressing-table in the bedroom and released her blonde hair, shaking her head to free it.

She unbuttoned her skirt, let it drop and

stepped out of it as she unbuttoned and pulled her blouse off, leaving her in her camiknickers.

It was very hot, despite the ceiling fan in the bedroom, and after the walk up from the gardens she was perspiring.

Biff couldn't take his eyes off her. It was still quite shocking being so *casually* in close proximity to a woman in her underwear, particularly a good-looking one like Rosemary.

In all his previous life he'd never so much as seen his sister in anything but her bedrobe.

Once some boys at school had got hold of a very daring fashion magazine from Paris. Inside there had been photos of models in *lingerie*. They had all savoured the word, practising their best French so that even the French mistress would have approved. There was even some speculation as to what she wore beneath her formal grey suit and black gown; after all, she was *really* French.

But now, here was his wife, after only a few days of marriage, unashamedly undressing before him and parading about completely unconcerned. And he had thought *she* would be the shy one: everybody had said to be gentle and considerate!

She drew on her silk dressing-gown, quite aware of his interest and pleaded: 'I really do need to rest, darling.'

Biff jumped. 'Sorry.'

As she passed him she stretched up and gave him a peck on the cheek.

'Don't be — I like it.'

* * *

At six o'clock they started dressing for dinner — or rather, Rosemary did. He sat out on the balcony in his striped dressing-gown, smoking a cigarette and sipping a cognac.

The sun was low in the sky, the slopes of Vesuvius turning a hazy purple in the humidity.

Far off, in the slate-blue waters the grey shape of a cruiser, its menacing form somewhat softened by bunting was slipping towards Naples dockyard, shadowed by two destroyers.

Nearer, the paddle steamer was coming back from Capri, its two red funnels billowing black smoke, its white wake curving away as it turned in from its journey up the coast. And everywhere were the red and white sails of the local fishermen.

Beneath him the harbour was full of pleasure boats and crowds of excited chattering families walking up the hill into the town.

He finished his Craven A, stood up and went back into the room through the open french doors. Rosemary was at the dressing-table in her petticoat, using a powder puff on her creamy white shoulders.

'Ah, just in time to help me with my frock.'

She stood up and went to the massive wardrobe, her image flashing in the mirror on the door as she opened it. She took out a full-length dress, slipped the material off the padded hanger and stepped into it, pulling it up and pushing her arms through the sleeves.

'Fix it for me, darling.'

When he'd done so she turned around, eyes gleaming.

'Do you like it?'

The shot-silk peacock-blue material shimmered in the light, fitting her tightly until, just at the knees, it flared gently out.

The neckline was folded and swagged from shoulder to shoulder. Her blonde, straight hair was combed to one side, held by a diamond clip, with matching pendant earrings.

He shook his head in wonderment.

'You look magnificent.'

She beamed. 'Thank you.' She gave him a suggestive look. 'Flattery will get you everywhere — later.'

It didn't take him long to change. He did

his black tie up and drew on his dinner jacket, checking for his gunmetal cigarette case and wallet. He called out 'Right, ready.'

Rosemary gave a last puff of scent to her neck, picked up her beaded evening bag and joined him at the door.

When they entered the bar they saw Konrad and Anna by the white grand piano. The black pianist was playing and singing in his soft tenor voice.

They made their way over. Konrad looked up, caught sight of them first.

He was also in a dinner jacket, his blond hair contrasting with the blackness of his suit. Anna was in a white silk dress with a high neckline and padded shoulders. At the waist she had a tied belt of the same material, with two long tassels. The dress flowed straight to the floor. Her dark hair had been pulled back into a chignon, and a thick diamond bracelet caught the light as she waved.

Konrad exclaimed when he saw Rosemary: 'My God, you are beautiful.'

Biff looked Anna up and down, and thought he'd never seen a more stunningly elegant woman in his life, but just said: 'And so are you.'

She smiled and nodded. 'Thank you.'

'Let's celebrate our beautiful ladies with champagne.'

Konrad turned to the counter and ordered a bottle. Later, as they made towards a table Biff suddenly saw that there was no back to Anna's dress at all — she was naked from her waist to the ribbon at the nape of her neck. It was very daring.

Rosemary saw it at the same time.

'Anna, what an incredible dress.'

'Do you like it? I got it in Paris last year.'

The girls talked of fashion as they settled themselves into the chairs in the garden room. Anna set her bag on to her lap and got out her cigarettes, offering them to Rosemary. 'Would you like one?'

'Turkish? Would you mind if I don't? Too strong for me.'

Biff took one instead as Rosemary found her Marcovitch Black and Whites.

Anna pushed her cigarette into a small ebony-and-silver holder. Konrad produced his lighter. When the flame reached Biff and he was alight he said: 'Thanks.' He nodded at the lighter. 'That's very nice.'

Handing it to him, Konrad agreed.

'Yes, it was given to me by my father when I entered the cadet school.'

It was made of gun metal, like his case, but with a coat of arms and a Germanic scroll.

'Is this your family crest?'

Konrad pulled a face. 'Yes. We can trace

our ancestors back to the . . . ' he turned to Anna for help. 'How do you say it?'

'Twelfth century.'

'Yes, twelfth century, but,' he made a dismissive gesture, 'in the modern Germany we tend not to worry about these things.'

Biff gave it back. 'All the same, it's very nice.'

Rosemary blew out smoke, looking around. 'Is it fuller than usual or am I imagining it?'

The long room was indeed busy with people dotted among the palms, mostly in dinner and evening dress, but there was the odd uniform, both military and *carabinieri*, and one officer standing nearby wore the uniform of black with silver lapel-badges of bundles of sticks wrapped around an axe — the Roman sign of authority.

The man started to come towards them, and it suddenly dawned on Biff that it was the same chap who had been behind the reception desk, and who had taken their passports on their arrival. He reached them and nodded. 'Good evening, Mr Banks, Mrs Banks, Oberleutnant and Frau von Riegner.'

Konrad stood up and shook hands, so Biff got slowly to his feet and reluctantly did the same.

As he did so Konrad said to him: 'Allow me to present Signore Alfredo Franchetti of

105

the *Milizia Volontaria per la Sicurezza Nationale*.'

Suspiciously Biff said: 'You know each other, then?'

Konrad grinned. 'Oh yes, the *signore* welcomed us to Sorrento when we arrived. He must surely have met you, too?'

Biff nodded. 'Welcome? He still has our passports.'

Franchetti waved a hand dismissively. 'A formality I assure you — just for a few days.' He looked at both girls. 'May I compliment you, gentlemen: your ladies are the most beautiful here tonight. I know *Il Duce* would like to meet you all.'

'*Il Duce*?' Biff frowned.

'Yes.' Franchetti beamed. 'He has been staying on Capri, resting after his successful meeting with Prime Minister Chamberlain, Daladier, and, of course, Herr Hitler.' He bowed slightly in the direction of Konrad. 'It is good to see the agreement they signed is already bearing fruit in your friendship here today. *Il Duce* will tomorrow come here by boat before going on to Naples for a conference. We are holding a banquet in his honour.' Franchetti grinned. 'I would be delighted if you would all attend as my guests.'

Biff was taken aback. To meet a world

leader, even a fascist one, was something, and what with the joy at the Munich agreement . . . Then he remembered Abyssinia.

But the decision was taken from him as Anna said something in German to Konrad. She looked very serious. He seemed uneasy, said something in return but Anna shook her head.

Konrad sighed, turned to Franchetti. He spoke in English.

'My dear Alfredo, I'm so sorry but we have made other arrangements. We are booked into Amalfi for the night, leave first thing after breakfast. We want so much to see the beauty of your coastline.'

Anna joined in quickly with: 'Our English friends are coming with us — isn't that so?'

It was news to Biff and Rosemary, but she recovered first.

'Yes, yes of course. We have come a long way to see it.'

Fanchetti couldn't conceal his disappointment.

'Can you not postpone?'

Biff had cottoned on at last that Anna really didn't want to attend, and chimed in with: 'Impossible, I'm afraid, we can only go tomorrow.'

'I see.' Franchetti appealed once more to Konrad.

'*Il Duce* has brought about peace. Seeing you all together would have been a nice gesture — yes?'

Konrad was forced to say: 'I agree but . . . ' he shrugged.

With a bleak nod, Franchetti excused himself. When he'd gone Konrad and Anna exchanged subdued but obviously heated words in German, before Anna swung around to Rosemary.

'I'm sorry, but if I hadn't included you Franchetti would have asked you anyway and you probably would have said yes.'

Rosemary raised an eyebrow, so Anna explained.

'Franchetti only wanted us there so that he could present us girls to Mussolini, who has a certain reputation with the ladies. A rather animal one. It could have got difficult — embarrassing.'

Konrad frowned, but didn't argue.

'Really?' Rosemary was bewildered. 'I didn't know that.'

Anna snorted. 'Oh yes. Rumour has it that he addresses the crowds from the balcony of the Pallazzo Venezia, while out of sight he is servicing Clara from behind.'

Hearing a woman speak like that shocked Biff, but Rosemary screamed with laughter.

Sheepishly Konrad began to smile. 'It's

true — the *rumours* I mean,' he added hurriedly.

The champagne arrived. When the glass coupes had been filled Konrad, visibly cheering up, proposed a toast.

'*Il Duce.*'

Even though Konrad was winking, Biff didn't really want to respond, and he didn't, but he let his glass clink with the others because they were all happy again. The girls whispered and giggled as Konrad leaned forward.

'Biff, I insist we stay the night in Amalfi. It would be embarrassing to be seen around here, especially in the evening. He may well have us observed.'

Biff snorted. 'So what?'

Grimacing Konrad sipped his drink.

'It's perhaps easier for you. Do not forget Germany and Italy have been an axis — allies — since 1936. A report could be sent to my Admiral, noted in my records.'

'Oh.' Biff had, frankly, forgotten about Konrad the naval officer.

Rosemary tapped the ash from her cigarette. 'Well, I'd like to go. It sounds fun.'

Biff stared at her, then at both grinning girls.

He must have still looked unconvinced because Anna said: 'There you are, Biff. My husband wants you to go, your wife wants you to go, *I* want you to go — so we go. Yes?'

They all waited expectantly.

Biff sighed. 'So how do we make arrangements?'

The other three cheered, causing some people to turn and look at them.

'I'll do that immediately,' volunteered Konrad, and got up.

He went off, easing his way through the throng.

'Have you been to Amalfi before?' Rosemary asked Anna.

Anna shook her head. 'No, but I've heard all about it from a friend. I was hoping for a day visit, but honestly, this would be better and we could have a great time.'

They'd finished the bottle and the sommelier had directed his waiter to supply another one before Konrad came back, beaming.

'Well?' Anna was impatient to know.

'All fixed.' He sat down. 'We are going to stay overnight at the Hotel Cappuccini Convento. It used to be a nunnery. What is more, I have taken the liberty of booking us into an evening concert at the Villa Rufolo in Ravella, followed by dinner afterwards at the Villa Cimbrone next door.'

'*Konrad*,' snapped Anna. 'Perhaps Biff and

Rosemary won't want to do that. You should ask first.'

He turned to them. 'Sorry, I hope it is all right. The concerts on the terrace at Rufolo are renowned for their setting. It's where Wagner received inspiration for his opera *Parsifal*.'

'That's fine, we'd love to.' Rosemary was excited. 'Villa Cimbrone. I read something in the newspapers about that place, I'm sure.'

Biff was not really listening. He liked dance music — but a concert . . . ?

'Biff?' Konrad pressed. 'They do short selections of Wagner — and other pieces, of course.'

Wagner! But he saw both girls looking imploringly at him.

'Well, I'll give anything a try once.'

'Wonderful.' Anna clapped her hands in delight.

Konrad breathed a sigh of relief. 'You will love it, I promise. And we are very lucky. They had cancellations due to Mussolini's visit. Mussolini's party is coming here instead.'

Anna took up her cigarette holder. Her voice was sarcastic. 'Well, there you have it: good can come out of anything. What time shall we set off?'

'We should go early, before the streets get

crowded; they might close some of them,' said Konrad.

Anna inserted one of her cigarettes into the holder.

'Have you got a car for us?'

Konrad looked exasperated. 'Of course, my dear. I did *everything*. The concierge is laying on the car and driver, from an agency they use.'

'I've got it.' Rosemary's eyes sparkled. 'Villa Cimbrone is where Greta Garbo sought refuge with that famous conductor earlier this year. They were supposed to be having an affair.'

Anna accepted a light from a passing waiter, then lifted the holder from her lips.

'Leopold Stokowski.'

'That's him.' Rosemary was delighted. 'Oh, Konrad, it sounds terrific.'

'Biff knew that he'd just have to sit through the concert, there was no way that Rosemary could be put off now.

'We're all agreed then.' Konrad looked around. 'The dinner in the Cimbrone is exceptional. All to do with the music festival.'

To celebrate they drank another bottle of champagne, then went out to the restaurant on the terrace.

A small orchestra was playing on a platform against the hotel wall. Opposite was the balustrade and beyond the unseen ocean. A brightly lit liner was anchored off shore, and an Italian destroyer, lit overall.

They took their seats. Both Biff and Konrad had noticed the looks their wives had received as they moved amongst the tables.

The waiters fussed around them, placing their napkins on their laps and giving out the menus. Spring water from bottles was poured into tumblers containing ice and a slice of lime.

They took some time before they were ready for the head waiter, who stood with pencil at the ready.

As soon as their selections were known the sommelier moved in with the wine list. After some discussion they settled for two bottles of white and a red, all from local vineyards. The sommelier, wearing his chain and badge of office, assured them they were choosing well. 'You will not be disappointed.'

They were not.

The band was playing 'Smoke Gets In Your Eyes'. It was the perfect end, to a perfect day.

7

Biff suddenly realized that the high sheriff had sat down with everybody clapping around him. He joined in, not having heard a word for the past ten minutes.

The times when he drifted off into his own little world of the past were getting more frequent these days — and longer. Still, it was a world he preferred.

People looked out for each other then, especially when the war came. But since the sixties and the rise of the *right* to self-fulfilment, with no sense of an obligation to society: in short, *duty*; since the arrival of drugs, binge drinking, political correctness and compensation; of graffiti and litter and a lawlessness on the streets that had not been seen since the nineteenth century . . . he took a deep breath, tried to stop himself. His doctor had told him not to get so riled up.

But it was difficult. He loved England — still did, but if he was a young man now, would he stay?

And would he and this generation fight for it, as they had in the past?

Was it worth the sacrifice so many had made?

'Come on. Let's get you home.'

It was his daughter, her hair the colour of her mother's when he'd first met her.

She helped him down to the street. The car was only a few feet away, parked in what he called a 'spasy' spot, the term he and his wife had coined when she had first got her set of disabled badges, with his not long after.

Several people greeted him, and one man insisted on helping him into the front seat, even though he could manage that himself.

When he was settled his daughter dropped into the driving seat, strapped herself in straight away, and fired up the engine.

'I'm sorry I've got to rush you, Dad, but the kids are home at four and Bill is due back early. We're going to a stupid rotary celebrity night.'

He murmured: 'Oh, I'm ready for a little snooze, don't you worry.'

It was true, but the fact that the kids were 'home at four' made him grin inwardly.

The elder boy was nearly eighteen, and the younger one sixteen: great hulking lads who seemed to be perpetually eating. The elder one was due to go to Cambridge in the autumn, to read German and politics, and the younger one was doing Mandarin Chinese and Russian with a special tutor. He grunted, the noise lost as the car engine revved up. It seemed languages were in the genes, his daughter had left University College London with a degree in Italian.

He was living now in a nice little bungalow in the village where once they'd had a large house and a couple of acres.

It was a good village. They all knew him. He had resisted all efforts to get him moved to sheltered accommodation in the town, but had settled for a twice-daily visit by a nurse, and a lady who cooked him his one good meal a day. She hadn't been required today.

Once inside he tried to usher his daughter out.

'Go on dear, I'm fine now. Thank you for a lovely day.'

She fussed a little, getting his jacket and shoes off, finding his favourite cardigan and slippers and settling him into his chair. She turned on the television.

He kissed her once again, said no, he didn't need anything — no tea thank you, and then, with a last kiss on the top of his head, he was alone.

The first thing he did was lift the remote, and point it at the goggle-box.

Blessed silence descended as he killed the bloody quiz presenter in mid inane sentence.

He shut his eyes as tiredness ached in his bones. But it had been a wonderful day.

116

★ ★ ★

The wine flowed, the band played, and they were laughing the night away.

All of a sudden there was a booming explosion that made the table contents jingle. One or two girls cried out in fright, but suddenly the night sky was lit up as a firework burst into a hundred little flares of intense blue. It marked the start of the display. A lot of people left their tables and flocked to the balustrade, but they sat where they were, giving a cheer every time a rocket exploded in a pyrotechnic display of intense colour.

'Do they do this every week?' asked Rosemary.

Konrad shook his head. 'I expect it's in honour of *Il Duce*'s visit.'

He laughed. 'Do you think he's in that destroyer? He couldn't possibly see them from Capri?' He grinned and added 'Probably visiting Clara on board.'

Anna set her glass down.

'Every time there is a bang, he's probably making her very happy.'

Konrad frowned, but Anna lolled back in her chair and stuck out the tip of her tongue.

'He's an *animal*.'

She said it quite loudly.

Konrad sat up and looked around.

'Anna — please.'

She gave a throaty chuckle that Biff found very attractive.

'Oh, you big brave sailor.'

But Konrad wasn't playing along. He stayed quiet, shaking his head and saying to Biff, 'She doesn't appreciate the delicacy of the position.'

Anna snorted. 'It was you who brought up the subject.'

'My dear Anna, I know, but can you not keep your voice down?' he hissed.

But the firework display was commanding everyone's attention.

Rosemary decided to help by changing the subject — to one she wanted to know whether Anna had heard of or had any views or interest in.

'What do you think about our King — Edward the Eighth — abdicating for love?'

'Ah. You mean the Prince of Wales and Mrs Simpson?'

'Yes.'

Anna held her glass out for more champagne as the waiter came around amid the continuing pyrotechnics.

'Well, I think he should have been allowed to marry her as he wanted, but I admire him for putting love before *everything*. It is the best thing that can happen to men and women.'

Konrad was nodding, but said: 'I agree with the first part, but he should not have neglected his duty to his country. Don't you think, Biff? Where would we all be if we did not do our duty? It makes nations strong.'

If truth be told Biff had never been able to make his mind up about the now Duke of Windsor. But before he could reply Rosemary said: 'I agree. He should have put the country first.'

Somehow, without thinking, Biff said: 'Life isn't that simple, though, is it? He was — is — passionately in love. It's the strongest force in nature.'

'Thank you, Biff.'

He suddenly realized he was siding with Anna, against Konrad and Rosemary.

Rosemary made a face.

'Oooh — you old romantic you. I'd never have thought it.'

Biff detected a note of irritation.

The country had been bitterly divided over the constitutional crisis and subsequent abdication, and Rosemary had obviously been in the camp that backed the cabinet decision rejecting the King's proposal of a morganatic marriage. Which he thought was strange, given her usual indifference towards the strictures of society.

Edward VIII had been very popular with

the working classes, largely because of his war record and his concern for the poor and long-term unemployed.

Konrad said: 'But despite everything we liked him very much in Germany. His visit last year was a great success. It is a pity you were not able to keep him as King.'

There had been much talk that the Windsors were sympathetic to the Nazi Government of Herr Hitler. It occurred to Biff to wonder: if the abdication had not taken place, would the relations between the two countries be better?

It prompted him to say: 'There is a great fear of war again in England. The *Anschluss* in March was worrying, and now you've gone into the Sudetenland. You can see why we're worried, can't you, Konrad?'

Konrad nodded.

'Yes, I understand, but not with Great Britain. The *Führer* is a great admirer of the British Empire. Like me, he is an Anglophile to his bone marrow — believe me.'

He held his arms out in supplication, glass in one hand.

'Biff, I ask you, what advantage could be there in fighting with you?'

He answered his own question. 'None. We seek only to carve out a fair and honourable place for ourselves in Europe. All the

Führer's actions have been only to unite the German-speaking peoples — that's all.'

Biff shrugged.

'I sincerely hope you are right. Nobody in their right mind wants fourteen-to-eighteen again, surely? It was supposed to end all wars.'

Konrad nodded. 'Agreed. But since then my countrymen have been through abject misery; inflation was so bad that people were taking home their pay in wheelbarrows — if they had a job at all. Some starved to death. Terrible, terrible times.' He shook his head. 'The *Führer* has ended all that, and the rise of communism. Surely you can see that if the British people had gone through the same experience, they too would honour the man who transformed their fortunes, making them proud to be British again?'

Bill conceded the point with a nod, but didn't say anything.

The girls, who had been deep in conversation about 'Wallis', and 'David', suddenly realized that their men had gone off on another, more serious tack.

Frowning, Anna said: 'Not *now*, Konrad, for heaven's sake. You boys should not talk politics.'

Konrad protested 'We're talking history.'

Anxious to change the subject himself, Biff agreed.

'Yes, Anna, it's all water under the bridge. It's the future that matters. We must all hope we have learnt from our mistakes.'

'You two are so alike.' Rosemary drained her glass. 'It's unthinkable that you would one day be trying to kill each other.'

This had a very sobering effect.

They all went quiet, until eventually Konrad slammed his hand on the table. 'Let's have some more champagne. Waiter . . . '

He held up his arm and waved the empty bottle. 'Another one if you please.'

Despite all the problems with Germany, Biff liked Konrad as an individual very much. In other circumstances they could well have become big chums.

There was a lot of truth in what he had said. Biff realized he would have felt the same if Britain had been in such a mess, whether or not it had brought it upon itself, and somebody had raised it back to its former glory.

In fact, he was half-inclined to the notion that Britain was drifting, with huge social problems, and needed somebody like Herr Hitler, or even *Il Duce*, to take over for a few years. He chuckled at the thought: to take over democratically, of course.

With the sound of the cork popping out they relaxed back into their earlier light-hearted banter, and when the band returned and started playing again, Konrad was on his feet.

'Rosemary, will you dance with me?'

When she shot Biff a glance he added quickly: 'With your permission?'

Biff said: 'of course,' and got to his feet, offering his hand. 'Anna?'

She got up immediately and together they followed the others on to the floor. It was a slow foxtrot, Anna turned and held up her arms. As Biff placed his hand around her waist he suddenly remembered there was no dress there.

Her back was smooth, and cool, and it made him feel as if they were being very intimate, not helped by the fact that she snuggled up close to him. He was aware of her warm breath and musky scent.

They said nothing for a while, just moving to the music, until she whispered: 'You love Rosemary very much.'

It was a statement, not a question, but he answered all the same.

'I do. And I can see that it is the same with you and Konrad.'

She smiled and nodded. They didn't say anything more. Given another time, another place, they knew that they would have been drawn to one another.

Anna was very light on her feet. She began

to sing the melody softly, making him feel very good.

As they did a turn he caught a glimpse across the dance floor of Konrad and Rosemary. There was no doubt in his mind that they too were very happy in each other's company.

What strange quirk of fate had brought them all together now?

'Penny for them?'

He came to with a rush. Anna was looking at him, one eyebrow raised, a faint grin playing on her strong, beautiful face. He went bright red, and flustered: 'Sorry. Just thinking of something Konrad said.'

He gave her a playful squeeze. 'My God, your English is so good — where did you pick up that expression?'

She chuckled. 'I spent two years doing post-graduate English at Oxford. I learned plenty of vernacular in the pubs after work.'

It was his turn to laugh, but she continued to look quizzical.

'What was it that Konrad said that you found so interesting?'

Still red in the face, Biff realized he couldn't say what he had really been thinking.

'Oh, how he likes Herr Hitler for what he has achieved in Germany.'

To his surprise, instead of agreeing she

turned her nose up.

'Not all of us are so enamoured — that is the correct word, isn't it?'

He nodded. 'Yes, but I don't understand. I thought you would be in full agreement?'

She said nothing for a while, as if she were carefully selecting her words, not wanting to go against her new husband.

'He has done wonderful things — there can be no doubt about that. But I fear for the future — for my children — when I have them. Hitler is not a man to rest on his laurels. What will he do next? We are all enraptured by him at the moment and that includes nearly everybody, despite some misgivings about this business with the Jews.'

She grimaced. 'There are rumours . . . ' she shrugged. 'But it is now too late to influence anything. We can only pray.'

Her words shook Biff.

'But Konrad — how does he feel? Has he worries?'

She pursed her lips. 'Sometimes, but he would never say anything to you; he is a very loyal person, an officer of the old school. He is not in the Nazi Party, though, despite some pressure and worry about future promotion prospects.'

As the music finished Biff twirled her around.

'Thank you, Anna.'

They walked back hand in hand to the table. Konrad was already helping to seat Rosemary, holding her chair for her.

'Hey there, you two — what have you been talking about so earnestly? We saw you, didn't we, Rosemary?'

Rosemary nodded at Biff.

'We did indeed.'

Anna, surprisingly, coloured slightly.

'Oh nothing, just the future.' She glanced quickly at Biff for support as she lied. 'Wondered where we'd all be in ten years' time, didn't we?'

He nodded. 'Yes. All with young children by then, no doubt — and you Konrad, you'll be an admiral, of course.'

Konrad roared with laughter.

'Oh yes, and I'll be visited by my friend the air marshal.'

They all joined in the merriment as Konrad cut the end from a large cigar, but it was Rosemary who said: 'What a wonderful idea.'

Everybody looked at her blankly.

'I mean, why not meet here — in ten years' time. It would be fun to see how we've changed.'

Anna agreed. 'I think that is a very good idea, but it is a long time ahead.'

Konrad lit a match and began drawing the air through the cigar, its tip glowing fiery red with every inhalation. When he'd finished he waved the match out and dropped the blackened remains into an ashtray.

'What do you say, Biff? Good idea or not? Perhaps you won't want to see us again.' He gave a chuckle.

Biff grinned and picked up his champagne glass.

'Why not? To our meeting again.'

For the rest of the evening they danced with their partners, getting more and more sentimental.

Just after midnight Biff and Rosemary returned to the table but stayed standing.

'We are turning in now,' said Biff.

Konrad and Anna stood up.

'You lovebirds, eh? Can't wait to go to bed.'

Rosemary flushed at Konrad's observation, but still held on to her husband who grinned.

'No more than you two, I see.'

'Touché.' Konrad took Rosemary's hand and kissed the back of it as Biff lightly kissed Anna on both cheeks in the French style.

'We'll see you in the morning, then,' said Anna. 'We have the car coming at nine o'clock, don't forget.'

'We won't.'

They made their way to the hotel's ancient

lift with its cage-like doors. When they'd gone Konrad murmured to Anna: 'Nice people. I'm sorry that we may soon be on opposite sides.'

She stiffened. 'What do you mean? Do you know something?'

He shook his head and held his new wife tightly around the waist.

'No my dear, I do not, but . . . '

What he didn't say hung heavily in the air.

Involuntarily Anna shivered.

She had found in Rosemary a woman friend she truly got on with — who thought and acted so like herself. And soon they would be enemies? It was unthinkable. When they reached their room, and Konrad began to undress her, she found she was still troubled by what he had said. Only when he lifted her on to the bed did she push it from her mind.

But in the deep dark of the night her mind was troubled once again until sleep came at last — despite Konrad's snoring like a transatlantic liner's deep siren.

Biff had found Rosemary more passionate than ever. When they'd finished and were cuddling together she suddenly said from his chest, where she had laid her head.

'Darling, what do you make of the von Riegners?'

'What do you mean?'

'Well — do you really like them a lot? Despite, well, you know, their being German?'

He grinned unseen in the darkness.

'What's that got to do with it, sweetie? People are people, aren't they? I think they are delightful.'

She snuggled happily against him.

'I'm glad you think that, because I like them very much. I truly would like to see Anna and Konrad again.'

She would have liked to say more but suddenly she realized that his breathing had become slower, more regular. Like Anna in her room, she lay awake, wondering and worrying about the future as her husband was lost in the deep sleep of post-coital bliss.

They had breakfast in their rooms, but they met in the foyer of the hotel with some luggage, not all of it, as they would only be away for one night in Amalfi.

'*Wie gehts*,' called a very jolly Konrad. 'Have you seen the car yet?'

Biff shook his head and went with him to the door, leaving the girls to embrace.

'No, I haven't seen it. What is it?'

As soon as he stepped out into the open he could see what it was: a very large, drophead, six-seater Mercedes Benz.

'Good God,' exclaimed Biff. 'I thought

we'd hired a car, not a tank.'

Konrad slapped his hand on the wing and bellowed: 'Good German engineering — the best.'

He looked around to see that the driver was nowhere near as he added softly: 'Not a bloody Italian car that will break down.'

The driver and porter came out with a trolley of luggage and began fitting their cases on the drop-down boot lid, using strong leather straps to secure the load in place.

They took leave of the hotel with the smiling manager and a couple of his staff waving them off. The car weaved its way out through the streets of Sorrento, past the shops and little restaurants, gay with bunting.

There were already many carabinieri, troops, sailors and blackshirts out on the streets and in the squares.

They began to climb up the narrow road that hugged the coast. In the distance they could see Mount Vesuvius dominating Naples and its bay, before, with yet another tight bend of the road back on itself, it went out of sight.

Before them were the white limestone mountains, falling precipitously into the blue sea, the steep valleys clothed in pines and chestnut trees.

Little white houses perched on the cliff

sides, smothered with red bougainvillea flowing over their balconies.

In the far distance, where the blue of the sea blurred into a haze where it met the sky, they could see the grey-white hulls of three more Italian warships.

They roared around a blind bend, the driver operating the two-tone horn several times as a warning. A man on a donkey with a cart was coming down the other side. The beast flicked an ear but didn't alter its rhythm. They climbed and descended, always zigzagging as the narrow road skated the steep valley sides, going from the sea into the green folds of the hills, then out again, sometimes passing through short dark tunnels. The driver said something to Konrad who was sitting beside him. He turned and shouted above the roar of the wind.

'He says it's an old Roman road. Brilliant engineering, yes?'

In the back the two girls were sitting together, with Biff next to them on the sea side. Sometimes he was looking down some 800 feet to the sea breaking on the rocks far below. Only a few feet of road and a low wooden fence stopped them from going over. He preferred flying. When there was no direct linkage to the ground, something to judge the height, he felt fine. With this sort of thing, in the hands of a man he had never met before, he was, to say the least, tense. Konrad didn't seem to notice.

After what seemed ages, but in reality must have been half an hour or so, they slowed and the driver pulled into an observation area. Konrad was immediately out, opening the door and helping the girls.

They all stood looking down on the little town of Positano, with the green, blue and yellow majolica dome of the cathedral of St Maria Assunta.

The driver said something in Italian which Konrad translated for them.

'He says this is known in Italy as the Vertical Town — you can see why, can't you? The town's piazza is the beach apparently; there is nowhere else that's flat enough.'

'Look at all those steps.' Rosemary pointed at a path where they must have numbered a hundred or more.

Anna put her arm through Rosemary's.

'How would you like to live there, Rosemary? Everything up and down, up and down, getting the groceries, taking the children to school?'

Rosemary shook her head. 'It's so beautiful, but for a woman a nightmare to live in.'

They got back in the car and continued the journey to Amalfi, the little town that gave its name to the coast where they were staying that night.

They came to a village set on a precipitous narrow cliff called Furore.

'Reminds me of a Norwegian fjord.'

Konrad stood up in the moving car to get a better view down to the tiny beach and flowing stream.

Anna tugged at his trouser leg and shouted something in German that made Biff and Rosemary chuckle: there could be no doubt that it meant 'sit down you idiot'.

Further on they reached a small natural inlet where the sea sparkled with an added greenness.

Konrad turned around. 'The driver says they have found a place they call the *Grotto della Emeraldo* — that means the Emerald Cave. He says it's very beautiful to see, it shimmers with light coming through the water from an underwater chimney. Do you want to see it?'

The girls chorused: 'Yes, please.'

The driver pulled into the side of the road where it had recently been widened. They all got out and followed him to the top of a long flight of steps which led down to the sea.

When they entered the cave the girls' voices echoed off its limestone walls.

'It's extraordinary.' Rosemary squatted

down and placed a finger in the mirrorlike brilliance of the green water. A ripple spread out across the surface to the far side.

Biff said: 'It's like the Blue Grotto on Capri.'

'Only this one is green.' Anna was teasing him.

'All right, clever clogs.'

'Clever clogs?' Anna giggled. 'That sounds funny.'

He grinned. 'Never been called that in one of your Oxford pubs?'

She vigorously shook her head, hair swishing about.

'Never.'

Rosemary stood up. 'Don't be rude, Biff.'

He pulled a face. 'Oh, you girls are sticking together, are you?'

Konrad grinned. 'In that case we must also forge an alliance, eh Biff?'

Biff heartily agreed. 'We certainly must.'

He realized that what he had just said had implications beyond themselves, and he could see that Konrad understood that too.

They held eye contact for a second, then Konrad nodded, just the once.

The girls looked at each other, not understanding, and rolled their eyes at each other as if to say: 'You haven't a chance.'

Back in the car, breathless from the steep

climb, they renewed their journey, passing trees of beautiful lemons lining the roads.

When they reached their destination the road came into the town at sea level, beside a building that was the old arsenal of what had once been a maritime republic. Drawn up on the beach were rows of fishing boats, with high prows and single masts, each carrying one triangular sail when it was up, reminding Rosemary of Arab boats on the Nile.

The driver turned up a narrow street, Rosemary catching the name Porta della Marina, which meant the Shipway Gate said Konrad, and into the Piazza Duomo.

The driver brought the car to a halt as they all took in the façade of the cathedral of St Andrews.

It was Anna who spoke first.

'It is truly magnificent.'

At the top of a straight line of fifty-seven steps the portico of the Moorish arches led the eye up to mosaics depicting the Apocalypse of St John and the twelve disciples. Beyond the roof, topped by a crucifix, were the towering milky-coloured rocks, capped by densely-grouped green trees.

'Come on, we must see inside.'

The girls went ahead as the men followed, leaving their driver to fend off a crowd of children who were gathering around the car.

'Just a minute.'

Biff aimed his new Kodak camera.

Smiling, Rosemary and Anna clung to each other until there was an audible click as the shutter operated.

They spent nearly an hour in the twelfth century Arab-Norman duomo, especially admiring the cool, peaceful cloisters at the rear of the church.

When they came out again, blinking in the strong sunshine, Konrad said; 'We'd better check in to the hotel, then how about some lunch?'

The driver took the car up a steadily inclined road cut into the hillside, the via Annunziatella, until they reached a massive building that overlooked the town.

'It's a converted convent of the Cappucins,' explained Konrad as they pulled up in the courtyard.

Unlike their hotel in Sorrento, the rooms were sparsely but comfortably furnished, with high ceilings and whitewashed walls.

There was a wonderful view of Amalfi from the colonnaded terrace, where bougainvillea fell in waves from the balustrade.

They dined down on the shoreline. Rosemary was taken with the fish that swam in the clear water alongside the floating deck of the restaurant, splashing and swirling the water as they fed them titbits of bread.

The tables, covered in white cloths, were arranged beneath awnings striped in red, white and green, Italy's national colours.

They slept for the rest of the afternoon, but at five o'clock they were back in the car, climbing up the road that zigzagged inland, getting higher and higher until eventually it levelled out at Ravello.

They entered the Piazza Duomo, with its cathedral, stopping at the steps that led up to the massive bronze door. They were remarking on it when Konrad hurried them up.

'Come on, we haven't much time.'

He led them towards crowds entering through a rustic stone gatehouse with a square tower, down a hard-packed clay drive into the partly ruined Villa Rufolo.

They barely had time to take a quick look around the magnificent gardens and a larger stone tower which, it was claimed, had so inspired Wagner that it became the Castle of Klingsor in his opera *Parsifal*, before they had to take their seats, which were set out in an arc.

The orchestra, dressed in dinner jackets, was before them, with the sea as a huge backdrop. They were tuning up as a few stragglers hurriedly took their seats.

When the conductor in a white dinner jacket appeared up a staircase from the right, they all applauded.

As the first chord of the eighteenth variation by Rachmaninov on a theme of Paganini swelled up in the flower-scented air, Biff looked sideways.

Rosemary and Anna's faces were in profile; both women were lost in the music, one dark, one blonde. His eyes found Konrad sitting at the other end, who smiled as if to say: 'I know, so beautiful, we're so lucky.'

It was a magical moment, one that the men would remember for the rest of their days.

It was a short walk through more gardens full of camellias, bougainvillaeas, roses and lemon trees to the Villa Cimbrone. It had been, they were told, renovated only that century, in classical and medieval styles, by the man who was responsible for Big Ben, one Lord Grimthorpe.

But Rosemary was only excited by the fact that Greta Garbo had been there that year during her notorious 'fling', as she preferred to call it, with Leopold Stokowski the conductor.

The candlelit dinner, with a string quartet playing softly outside the room, on the terrace, was unforgettable. At the end of the evening they walked slowly back, Rosemary on the arm of Konrad, Biff escorting Anna.

'That was wonderful, Konrad.' Rosemary was sleepy, leaning heavily on him. 'Thank you for organizing it. We would never have done this on our own.'

He patted her hand with his and chuckled.

'Thank my darling wife, Anna. Her dislike of *Il Duce* was the reason.'

His wife was apologizing to Biff.

'I'm sorry — was the concert not to your liking — were you bored?'

He shook his head violently.

'Not at all, whatever gave you that idea?'

Anna smiled, her face caught in the light from the lamps along the path.

'I thought you were asleep at one point.'

They were holding hands. He felt close enough to her to lift it and gave it a mock slap.

'You were mistaken. I was letting the music flow over me.'

She giggled.

'I could see that.'

They drove back down the hill, still with the roof off, the warm night air full of the scents of the unseen trees and bushes, their yellowish headlights picking out fluttering moths and the occasional black shape of a bat. As they came into Amalfi Biff turned in the front seat and looked back. Konrad was in the middle, the two girls slumped with a head on each shoulder, both fast asleep.

He grinned, but by the time they got to the hotel the girls had begun to stir.

Biff got out first and opened the door for Anna. She was dreamy, so he leaned in and gently pulled her to her feet. She stumbled into him, and he had to steady her with his arm around her waist for a moment. He was conscious of her warmth, her softness, her perfume and the reaction of his body.

Konrad got out. 'Thank you, Biff,' he said, and Anna snuggled up against him as Biff hurried around to the other side and helped a blinking stretching Rosemary. He felt guilty, as if he had been unfaithful to her, but he knew that that was being stupid.

It was not every day that an attractive young woman fell into his arms.

'Come on, old girl, let's get you to bed.'

Anna must have woken up a little, because she giggled.

'You English. If he called me an 'old girl' I'd hit him.'

Konrad made a face of horror.

'I wouldn't dare, my darling.'

Biff sniffed.

'Yes, well, it's a way we English have of showing our affection.'

'Funny way.' Anna was staggering a little as they walked into the hotel. Biff realized she had drunk an awful lot of wine — both of them had, only with Rosemary it had made her quiet — up to now.

They got their keys from the desk, the girls making a noise one moment, excessively shooshing with forefingers to lips the next.

Their rooms were adjacent.

Konrad and Biff opened the doors with their keys, keeping one hand on their swaying and still shooshing wives.

For the first time Anna had a slight accent.

'Now be a good boy, Biff, my friend wants to go to sleep, don't you, Rosemary?'

Rosemary gave her a huge wink, and they fell into each other's arms, whispering loud enough to be heard by anybody standing yards away.

Anna said 'You call me, Rosemary, if you need help — pilots can be very demanding when they are at the controls.'

Rosemary seemed to think that was very funny.

'And you too, Anna. Don't let him torpedo you when you are not looking.'

They went off into gales of laughter, which their menfolk did not find amusing, pulling them apart and pushing them quickly into their rooms.

Konrad and Biff shook their heads in mock despair.

'A great day, Konrad,' said Biff. 'Thank you.'

'It was good, *ja*? See you in the morning.' With that they followed their young wives into their rooms and gently closed the doors.

The only sound that could be heard in the corridor after that was the odd girl's voice giggling with pleasure, and the rhythmic creaking of ancient springs.

To Biff's bewilderment at first, a tipsy Rosemary had insisted on facing the pillow, rearing and pushing back at him like a young mare. But then, with increasing pleasure and forcefulness he held her by the nape of the neck as she enjoyed herself immensely, pretending to be a long-maned, highly strung and proud arab steed being broken in by her master.

After that she crashed out and slept for ten hours straight, leaving a shaken Biff to open the window and smoke a cigarette, looking at the lights of the town below, and hearing the waves breaking on the faraway cliffs. He decided that he wasn't a pervert after all, and that he'd like to do that again please.

8

The girls wore sunglasses and headscarves in the morning, and only really started to come to life after a stop for coffee and cakes on the journey back to Sorrento.

Anna shook her hair free first, and then as Rosemary laid her sunglasses on the café table, said: 'I'm sorry — did I misbehave last night?'

Rosemary removed her scarf. 'No more than anyone else.'

She shot a guilty glance at Biff, who pretended to be interested in Konrad throwing stones into the sea from the shingle beach before them.

Anna's face lightened.

'Oh — good. I'm afraid I can get carried away sometimes. I didn't mean to drink so much. It just happened. I was having such a good time.'

Rosemary nodded. 'I know just what you mean.'

As the coffee cups and saucers were laid out, and a plate of cakes set down, Anna said 'Honestly, I feel I've known *both* of you since . . . childhood.'

'Isn't that strange. I feel that way too.'

Rosemary was genuine; in Anna she had a friend she had chimed with immediately. She could easily convince herself that she had been at school with her, the bond felt so strong.

Biff nodded at Konrad who had started back towards them, coming up the steps to their table.

'I must admit, he is like the brother I never had.'

'Brother?' Anna chuckled. 'That would make you my brother-in-law — yes?' Konrad slumped into a chair beside her.

'Biff your brother-in-law? How is that?'

Before Anna could answer an embarrassed Biff said:

'I was just saying, you're like a brother.'

Konrad grinned and gave him a punch on the arm.

'I agree. Brothers — just so. We should see more . . . ' he stopped abruptly, his face clouding. 'But we live in difficult times. We should not forget that.'

Biff looked intently at him.

'How do you mean?'

With his blond hair bright in the sunshine Konrad took a second before replying, conscious that they were all looking at him.

'All I mean is, the world is restless, is it

144

not?' He gestured at Biff.

'No doubt you will have to leave England and go and fight somewhere in your Empire, India or Iraq, perhaps? And I for my part will probably leave my comfortable, boring job with the admiral; it must soon come to an end, and I could be floating off the coast of Africa, or Russia or some other god-forsaken place in a few months' time.'

No one replied immediately, the only sound was of the sea lapping on the beach. Biff found Rosemary's eyes. They were troubled.

He stirred himself.

'Well, we chose to be sailors and airmen didn't we, Konrad? Presumably because we didn't want to be in offices all our lives.'

Anna laid a consoling hand on Rosemary's.

'Don't worry — look at these two. They will be all right.'

She glanced at Konrad. 'What do you think you are doing, depressing everybody?'

He attempted to be jolly, rolling his eyes.

'Sorry. I shall leave that to you as usual.'

They welcomed the arrival of the coffee, joking again as Anna poured and handed round the cups. After the cake they all enjoyed a cigarette before getting back in the car and heading for Sorrento.

But they lapsed into silence, broken only by

the occasional remark at some passing scenic splendour.

Konrad had caused a heaviness in all their hearts, put into words at last by Rosemary, looking across at Anna.

'When do you go back?'

Anna frowned. 'What day is today?'

'It's Monday.' Konrad had heard them and turned round in his front seat. 'And we leave Saturday.'

'Oh.' Anna's face fell.

Both girls looked at each other.

'Only four more days.' Rosemary was crestfallen.

Biff tried to cheer her up.

'So let's make sure we do things together from dawn to dusk.'

Konrad chimed in, trying to dispel the gloom that he had instilled in them all.

'We drink champagne and we eat and we dance — every night.'

As the car started to weave through the streets of Sorrento, past road sweepers cleaning up from Mussolini's visit, it was decided. They would go to Capri, they would swim, more tennis, and visit the town for shopping and lunch together.

By the time they turned into the hotel's drive they had cheered up a bit. As they collected their keys and prepared to separate, they agreed on a time to meet out by the pool.

'After the tennis competition, we shall now have a Germany against England swimming match,' announced a beaming Konrad.

In their room Biff untied his canvas shoes, took them off and collapsed on to the bed. Disconsolately Rosemary kicked hers across the floor, then flung herself down beside him.

'Oh Biff, isn't it sad? We won't ever see them again, will we?'

Biff put his arm around her.

''Course we will, darling.'

But in truth, he realized that what Konrad had been trying to say was true. Whether or not there was a war in Europe, it would be difficult for them to pretend that they would be able to see each other regularly in the next few years, but he tried to cheer her up — and himself.

'We might be able to arrange something, we shall have to see. I'll have a word with Konrad.'

She snuggled up to him.

'Oh darling, would you? I'm so fond of Anna I can't begin to tell you how much I'm going to miss her when they go. It's so unfair. I know I've got all my friends at home, but Anna is just — well, we think the same way, we laugh at the same things.'

He gently stroked her hair.

'I know, darling, I know. Konrad could be one of the chaps in the squadron.'

He meant to convey that he would trust him with his life.

They were the first down at the pool, Biff diving in and doing a length and back before pulling himself out, his grey wool bathing-trunks heavy with water.

Rosemary looked beautiful in a one-piece dark-blue costume with a thin white belt.

'I'm not going in until Anna gets here.' She waved her rubber bathing-cap in the air. 'Speak of the devil, here they are.'

Biff turned. Konrad was in a tighter, racier pair of trunks that made Biff feel positively old-fashioned.

But it was Anna whom he couldn't take his eyes off — or rather he did, but it was a struggle.

She was slender, a little less curvy than Rosemary, but her shoulders were square and athletic, and her dark hair was shown up by the white swimming-suit made of some shiny material.

'Gosh, you both look terrific.'

'Flattery will not get you anywhere,' laughed Anna as she pulled on her rubber cap and pushed up errant dark curls under its edge.

'We are going to beat you in revenge for the tennis.'

And they did, though Konrad and Biff were virtually equally matched, the former just getting his nose ahead on the last lap of the five they had set themselves.

As they stood side-by-side, arms on the pool edge, Konrad wheezed.

'You sure you are not in the Royal Navy, Biff?' He shook his head. 'You swim like a fish.'

Biff had his little finger in one ear, trying to get the water out.

'Not as good as you though, you're more like a destroyer the way you cut through the water.'

Konrad grunted. He almost said something but changed his mind.

Rosemary had ordered a bottle of champagne on their bill; the waiter, already briefed, brought it out in a bucket of ice dressed with ribbons and a bit of greenery which was supposed to be laurel.

'To the victors — the swimming team from Germany — we present this trophy,' Biff called aloud as the girls clapped. Heads turned, and a large man got up and ambled over with his camera, gesturing for Konrad and Rosemary, now with her cap off and blonde hair free, to stand on either side of the 'trophy'.

Konrad frowned, spoke in German to the man, who said something, and then looked quite surprised as Konrad gave a laugh, shaking his head.

Puzzled, Rosemary asked Anna,

'What did the man say?'

Konrad pointed to Anna, then beckoned her to stand beside him and Biff to go with Rosemary, all the time addressing the man with the camera.

Anna chuckled. 'He is another German, Konrad met him earlier on. Very boring, a member of the Nazi Party and he doesn't let you forget it.'

Frowning, Rosemary said: 'I still don't understand?'

Anna turned to her, eyes alive with amusement.

'He thought you were Frau von Riegner, not me, because you are so Aryan looking — with your blonde hair.'

'Oh.' Rosemary didn't know whether to be flattered or not.

Anna stood with Konrad, the 'trophy' in front of them, as the man held his camera steady and took a photograph.

There was another exchange in German, in which 'English' was mentioned.

'He wants to take one of you two now.' Anna gestured for them to stand together.

They were duly photographed, and then, with further joking and guffaws, they were photographed again, this time Konrad with Rosemary, and Biff with Anna. The man, who was of massive build, shook them all with a hand the size of a dinner plate before ambling back to his seat.

'He is going to get his film developed tomorrow and he says he will give us a copy each, isn't that nice of him?'

Konrad was trying hard to keep a straight face. 'He is very difficult to refuse, yes?'

The champagne was popped as Rosemary whispered to Anna: 'Still, they will be nice to have, won't they?'

That night they dined out in the town, in a garden of olive trees, under fairy lights and a full moon. They decided to walk home, Konrad escorting Rosemary, Biff with Anna on his arm.

They stopped at a point where the road ran by the sea and, from a cliff top, looked at the moonlight shining on the water.

Nobody said anything. It would have spoilt the moment.

In the morning they caught the steamer to Capri. Whilst the girls sat in deckchairs and talked the two men walked the deck, taking in the salt-laden breeze and the hiss of the waves as they washed down the side of the boat.

They ended up in the prow, looking at the mountainous island that was Capri, with at one end the sheer drop into the sea where the Emperor Tiberius had had people thrown to their deaths from his villa.

They docked at the *marina grande* and took an open-topped 'Capri taxi' up the steep road that repeatedly bent back on itself, time and time again, until they reached the higher town.

After wandering the alleyways they ended up in a little square, and celebrated with some pasta and a bottle of Chianti, before returning to the boat and sailing back again.

Standing in the stern, Biff watched the island recede, white in the sun . . . white . . . white . . .

★ ★ ★

When he looked up he was surprised to see the nurse in her white overall looking down at him.

'Mr Banks. Mr Banks. Come on, my love, it's time to get you ready for bed.' She never stopped talking as she got him to the bedroom and helped him undress and get into his pyjamas.

Biff found himself in the bedroom being told in the nicest possible way: 'Now don't forget to brush your teeth properly.'

She bustled off to fix his evening medicines.

Fumbling as he squeezed out the striped paste on to his brush, he grumbled aloud: 'Told to clean your teeth when you were eight and still being told, eighty years later.'

After he'd done them and rinsed out, he splashed his face with the cold water.

She was ready for him, plumping up his pillows and helping him into bed.

'Now, are you quite sure you wouldn't like something to eat? I could make you a sandwich.'

He shook his head.

'No thank you. I've eaten far too much today already — and besides,' he flashed her a look of triumph, 'I've already cleaned my teeth.'

She shook her head in good-natured annoyance and clicked her tongue.

'So you have. Well, here are your pills.' She handed him a tumbler of water and loudly counted them out. 'One, two, three?' as he swallowed them.

'I can count, thank you very much.'

She ignored him; he was slightly cantankerous that evening. She'd got to know his moods pretty well over the last few months since she'd been brought in after the death of his wife. Normally pleasant, she had noticed recently that he had seemed absent at times, at others very slightly irritable. She would report it to the doctor, perhaps there was some slight brain pathology? She kept her mind open though, he was allowed to be grumpy at eighty-eight.

She made sure he had his alarm call button around his neck before spending a few more minutes going around the house making sure everything was secure. He heard her tidying up in the kitchen before she came back into the bedroom.

'Well, I'll be off now. You've got everything — water, tablets?'

She made the motions of tucking him up, and turned on the television.

He nodded. 'I'm fine.'

Although she was a professional to her fingertips she had grown very fond of him.

'See you in the morning then.'

He said goodbye, listening as she slammed the front door, pushing at it several times to make sure it was shut.

He turned off the television immediately.

Silence descended.

He turned to his combined alarm clock and CD player and selected a disc from a small rack of favourites.

When he was sure it was running he turned

off the light. The room was plunged into blackness, which slowly resolved into shapes picked out by the faint light coming from the curtained window. It had to be a full moon out there.

The crooner's soft voice floated in the room backed by the muted saxophones. It was recorded in 1938.

★　★　★

Biff and Anna moved slowly around the room, her head on his shoulder as they swayed to the music.

It was their last night, out on the terrace, the orchestra in white DJs, the tables lit by little red lamps, the moon on the wane, but still bright above a placid ocean. Konrad and Rosemary were sitting the dance out and she had moved to be beside him, their blond heads close together as they talked.

Anna whispered in Biff's ear.

'It's very sad — parting, isn't it?'

He nodded. 'We shall miss you.'

When the dance ended he led her back to the table.

She sat down next to Rosemary who mournfully said: 'I can't bear to think that you are off in the morning and we shan't see you again.'

Anna leant forward, forearms on the table, a finger stabbing at the white cloth. She looked around at them all.

'No, let's meet again this time next year.'

She saw the doubtful looks in Konrad's and Biff's eyes, and added, frowning:

'All right, I know it may be difficult, but we will try every year until we do.'

Rosemary clapped her hands with enthusiasm. 'Yes, and after five years, that would be in . . .'

'October nineteen forty-three,' grunted Biff.

'Yes, then we make a very special effort.'

Triumphantly Anna added, eyes flashing challengingly at the boys: 'And if all else fails — even in October 1948, we *must* do it, we *must* meet again.'

'We will,' said Rosemary firmly. 'Let's exchange addresses right now.'

With paper and pen supplied by the waiter they busied themselves with writing. Anna said as she finished with a flourish: 'We live in Hamburg — and you?'

Rosemary showed her the address, pointing with her pen at the paper. 'We've rented a cottage. It's in a little village in Essex called Tolleshunt D'Arcy — not far from London, about thirty minutes by train.'

Biff and Konrad must still have been

showing their unease, because Anna turned on them, especially her husband.

'What is it *now*?'

There was a glint in his wife's eye that Konrad already knew so well.

'All right, all right, I want to meet this Englishman again very much.'

He gave a playful punch to Biff's stocky shoulder. Not to be outdone Biff ruffled the German's hair.

'And I want to see him again before he goes bald.'

They spent the rest of the evening talking about their holiday, and their time on the Amalfi trip. When they noticed that they were the last ones, that the orchestra was already packing up, they stirred themselves.

'What time do you leave tomorrow?' asked Rosemary, as she and Anna walked slowly arm in arm.

'We have a taxi booked for seven o'clock.'

'We shall come down to see you off.'

Anna shook her head.

'No, Rosemary, it's far too early to be getting up on your holiday. We will say goodbye now.'

'No — I won't hear of it.'

Whilst the girls argued Biff and Konrad walked quietly behind them.

'Well, it's come at last.'

Konrad nodded at the girls. 'Whatever they decide, I'd like to say goodbye quietly — now.'

Biff nodded. 'Take care of yourself, Konrad.'

'And you too, Biff.'

They glanced knowingly at each other.

In the event, after a restless night, Biff and Rosemary were up and in the foyer of the hotel before Konrad and Anna appeared, watching as their trunk and cases were hauled out of the lift by the porters.

Eventually Anna came down the stairs, dressed in a grey suit with a fox fur draped around her shoulders, a little netted hat on her head.

It seemed strange seeing her in the everyday wear for a colder climate. They had only ever seen each other on holiday, and dressed appropriately.

'Darling, you look wonderful.'

Anna pulled a face. 'Thank you, Rosemary.'

The taxi was already outside, the luggage being loaded by the porters. As the girls walked towards it they promised to write to each other as soon as they got home.

Konrad appeared, immaculate in a double-breasted tweed suit, an overcoat over his arm, a feathered Tyrol-style hat on his head. He and Biff followed the girls out and stood for a moment, everybody looking silently at the others, then the girls hugged, and Anna turned to Biff and gave him a kiss on the cheek, her hand lightly touching his, as Rosemary did the same with Konrad.

Then it all happened so quickly. Biff shook Konrad's hand; next thing the German couple were in the car, doors slammed and it was on the move, turning, then heading up the drive.

They could see Anna waving through the small back window, then they were gone.

Disconsolately they made their way into breakfast, hardly speaking. As if in sympathy with their mood the morning was grey, with a hint of rain in the air.

'It is late now,' said the waiter apologetically. 'The season is almost over.'

It matched their mood.

And, like their mood, in the remaining few days it never was as bright and sunny again.

9

The little thatched cottage stood a mile from the airfield. Having obtained permission to live out of mess, he bicycled to it every day. On most mess dining-in nights he stayed on station, having once gone arse over tip into a ditch on the way home. Fortunately, he fell with all the naturalness of the drunk and only suffered scratches from the brambles.

After their arrival Rosemary did nothing for a week, except for sending a postcard of the village to Anna and Konrad; then boredom drove her to get a job as a secretary with a local estate agency — the one that had found the cottage for them.

Every night, after supper, they sat in front of a log fire, talking. When the photographs were developed Rosemary was delighted and put one showing them all in a frame on the stone mantelpiece.

She wrote again to them, this time a letter on her office typewriter, calculating that it would be easier for them to read, conscious that it was in English.

She put some photographs in the envelope as well, got it weighed and bought stamps at the local post offiice, The woman gave her a funny look, especially when Rosemary took the letter back again, deciding that Biff ought to read it before it was sent.

He did, as Rosemary in her apron bustled around the kitchen. She put the pot of stew and dumplings on to the table.

'That's fine.' He folded it up and sealed it down.

'I'll send it in the morning.'

As they ate he told her of his day and of the excitement because tomorrow he was at last going to fly the 280 mph Blenheim.

'You will be careful, won't you, darling?' Rosemary drawled, without looking up from her work. Obviously she had complete faith in his abilities.

In the event, on the next day he found that the training on the Anson had paid off. Under the watchful eye of his instructor he eased the throttles forward, and taxied the Blenheim to the end of the runway, turning into the wind when the control tower gave permission.

After running up the engines and checking the magnetos he finally let her go, and climbed into the bright autumn sky.

At last, he was a pilot on a front-line squadron.

His elation was short-lived. As he walked

back across the grass pulling off his helmet an aircraftsman ran up and saluted.

'Sir. The adjutant would like to see you as soon as possible.'

Puzzled and a little apprehensive Biff hurried to the adjutant's office. The tall, elegant old Etonian who sported a monocle had been a pilot in the Great War, and was nearing the end of his service. On certain days — days that obviously meant something to him he — he dressed in the khaki uniform of the old Royal Flying Corps, with breeches and Sam Browne. Biff saluted.

'Ah Biff, come in, come in, take a pew.'

It all seemed friendly enough.

'Sir?'

It was then that he saw the letter to Konrad and Anna lying on the desk.

He frowned, what was it doing there?

The adjutant saw that he had seen it, and picked it up.

'Yes. You left this in the squadron post office this morning?'

Biff nodded. 'Yes sir. My wife typed it at work but brought it home for me to read before we posted it. Is there a problem?'

The adjutant offered his cigarette case. Biff took a Passing Cloud and accepted a light. He was getting uneasy but the older man took a long pull on his cigarette, holding it affectedly in the gap between his second and third fingers, exhaling the smoke before he answered.

'There could be.'

He leant back in his chair.

'Biff, we might be at war with the Hun again sometime soon.' It was strange hearing the term 'Hun' — so old fashioned, 'and here you are, a serving officer sending letters to Germany. Can you not see that it could be misconstrued?'

Biff felt the floor dropping out beneath him.

He spluttered. 'Sir, I'd never pass on any information — surely you believe me?'

When nothing was said he reached for the letter.

'You want me to open it?'

Before he could do so the adjutant barked: 'No.'

He relented, said gently: 'No, Biff, that will not be necessary, but you can see the difficulty, can't you? Others might not be so trusting.'

Miserably Biff shrugged.

'It was on holiday. They were very good people, sir — became great friends. It will break my wife's heart if we can't keep in touch.'

'Hmm.'

The adjutant tapped the ash into his tray made from a piece of gearing.

'Nobody is suggesting that you can't keep on writing to them, but you should be apprised of a couple of points.'

He held up the fingers of his free hand and grasped the first. 'One — we will have to inform higher up — and you may get a censure, or,' he looked expectantly at Biff, 'other people might be interested, who will perhaps want you to include various bits of information, or should I say *misinformation*.'

Biff got the implication, but before he could explode with indignation and say he would do no such thing to Konrad the adjutant moved to his next finger.

'Two: your friend may be a great fellow, but he is the servant of a totalitarian state, and may well be subject to greater strictures — and pressures — than you.'

Helplessly Biff said: 'So, what do you want me to do?'

The adjutant shrugged. 'That's up to you. I just thought you ought to know.'

He realized then that the old boy was taking care of him, making sure he didn't get into trouble: his squadron — his family.

He looked at the letter for a moment, then pushed it with one finger towards the adjutant.

'As I said, they're good people. I'll risk it.'

He told Rosemary who was suitably outraged.

'My God, if I'd posted it they would never have known.'

Biff had been thinking about it.

'I'm not so sure.'

She looked up sharply from the floor, where she had been kneeling, using the poker, raking the ash in the grate with a vengeance.

'What do you mean?'

'I think there's a strong possibility that all correspondence with Germany is being monitored — and vice versa.'

'Oh.' Rosemary sagged back on to her heels. 'Is it that bad?'

He didn't reply. They stayed numbly silent for some time.

At last she said: 'I can't help worrying about Konrad and Anna.'

He nodded slowly. 'And for all of us.'

They had a great Guy Fawkes night, scuffling through the mounds of dead leaves to reach the village green. As the bonfire blazed, and Guy Fawkes's head rolled off, potatoes were placed at the edges to be raked out later.

Fireworks screamed and banged, jumped, spun and whooshed into the night sky.

Children ran everywhere, faces alive with excitement caught in the light from the flames. Biff held Rosemary in front of him, arms wrapped protectively around her.

Two days later the papers were full of the smashing of hundreds of Jewish shop windows all across Germany — an event the leader columns called the *Kristallnacht*. The Jews were also forced to wear a yellow star of David on their clothes.

It was mid December before a letter was on the mat when Rosemary came down the tightly turning wooden staircase, still half-asleep. She picked it up, turned it over. In her befuddled state it was a second before she took in the fact that it was from Germany.

Feverishly she rushed to the kitchen, used a knife to slit it neatly open.

The first things that she saw were the photographs: one of her and Konrad that the big German had taken, then one of all four of them at Amalfi taken by a waiter, and lastly another of Anna and Biff.

Fumbling she opened out the letter and began reading.

It was from their address in Hamburg.

Dear Rosemary and Biff,
Thank you so much for your letter and the

great photographs — it was wonderful to hear from you again.

I'm so sorry it has taken this long to write to you, but my mother was taken ill on the day we got back to Hamburg — sadly she died two weeks ago. It is only now that I have managed to get back to normal, having nursed her all this time.

I do so miss you both, and the wonderful time we had together in sunny Italy. The weather is so cold and wet here — is it the same for you?

Konrad has got a sea appointment now, so I have been on my own — with my mother that is — these past weeks.

Is Biff well? Doing a lot of flying I expect with his squadron? Do you live near the airfield?

There was lots more. Rosemary sank into a chair, a finger curling the hair on her forehead as she read on.

But the last paragraph was the best.

I'm sure we shall be able to meet again soon. Maybe in Spain this coming summer? We could rent a house and enjoy wine and sun together, like before. Let us know how you feel, and we'll start planning.

I look forward to hearing from you

— please write again soon.
We love you both.

Anna and Konrad.

Stupidly Rosemary's eyes started to well up with tears. She knew it was probably her condition; they'd only just found out she was expecting, but she did so miss them.

It was not long afterwards that Biff was called to the CO's office, to be confronted by a man in a pinstripe suit, called Mr Chandler, and the CO who told him to take a seat.

Biff did so, conscious of their eyes on him. The man called Chandler spoke first.

'Flying Officer Banks, you received a letter from Germany about a week ago?'

He nodded. 'Yes sir — from friends we met on holiday.'

So that was it.

His jaw dropped at what was said next.

The man in the pinstripe suit suddenly said:

'In it you were asked, did you live near the airfield, were you flying a lot with your squadron? About the weather, and tentative plans to meet in Spain, presumably near Gibraltar? Is that so?'

Biff was both amazed and angry. He appealed to his CO.

'Sir, that's outrageous. This man must have opened our private mail.'

Obviously embarrassed the CO brushed the back of his hand over his moustache.

'I'm sorry, Banks, but these are troubled times. Mr Chandler here is . . . ' he shot him a glance and the man nodded, 'from MI5.'

Chandler murmured. 'Don't take it personally, Banks. You are a serving officer. You must see that you could well be targeted — compromised?'

'Sir, with great respect, I give you my word, Konrad and Anna von Riegner are tremendous people, they are not Nazis. I would trust them with my life.'

Chandler sat down on the corner of the CO's desk, swinging one leg. 'I'm sure they are. But you must realize that the Germany they live in, Herr Hitler's Third Reich, is not a pleasant place. They may be under some . . . ' he paused, 'shall we say *guidance*, when it comes to writing to you.'

Miserably Biff made no reply. The adjutant had tried to warn him.

Chandler said:

'All that is required of you is that when you write again, you provide, casually of course, some photos and information . . . about your squadron. We could help you there, say it's larger than it is, something on that line, nothing special. Would you do that? You can carry on your friendship. Heaven,' he gave an oily grin, 'my mother's grandfather was a Jerry, so that makes me a bit of one too, eh?'

Chandler's face tried to smile, but there was no warmth in his eyes.

'You don't mind do you?'

Biff pulled his chin into his chest and looked back defiantly.

'And if I do?'

'Come now, Flying Officer, that's hardly the attitude to take by one holding His Majesty's commission.'

Biff shot an angry glare at the CO and back to Chandler.

'And I would remind you — *Sir* — that His Majesty is also of German descent. They are not all Nazis.'

There was an awful silence. Perhaps he'd gone too far. He finally shook his head resignedly.

'I tell you again, you've got it wrong. They are good people.'

The CO came to his aid.

'I'm sure they are, Banks, it's just that there are greater issues at stake. We've all got to do our bit for the country — however distasteful.'

Chandler's smooth voice continued as if there had been no interruption.

'You've only known them since your honeymoon, is that correct; a chance meeting, I gather.'

He made 'chance' sound highly suspicious, highly unlikely.

Biff just glared back at him and made no attempt to answer.

When he told Rosemary she went off her head, shouting and crashing around the kitchen, finally banging the plates of liver and onions on to the table.

'It's outrageous — opening people's mail. What sort of a country have we become? And they have the nerve to carry on about Germany.'

She sat down again and pulled her chair violently up to the table, its legs screeching on the floor.

'Biff, I absolutely refuse to play along with this. You do what you like, but I shall write back myself, and the letter won't go anywhere near your damned airfield.'

He swallowed, guessing that they would know about it one way or the other. If they thought he was deliberately trying to avoid them, would it affect his career in the air force? To hell with it. He got up, went to her and put his arm around her.

'You do that, darling. Konrad and Anna mean more to us — deserve more from us than any of them.'

Out of character, she suddenly burst into tears.

Biff was taken by surprise. He found a handkerchief so that she could wipe her eyes and blow her nose.

'I'm so sorry, Biff. It's the pregnancy I expect. I get so worked up about things lately — and this is the last straw. Who are they to spoil our friendship by making all these horrible assertions?'

He crouched down before her, knowing it was not the time to say they were only doing their job — protecting the country and all that. Instead he kissed her temple and ran a soothing hand over her hair, which she was growing longer.

'Only we know how close we are to them, darling, and we shall be close for the rest of our lives — long after any of the present difficulties are over and long forgotten. Young Biff here,' he ran a hand gently over her tummy, 'will stay with them every summer, become bilingual, and their sprogs will come over here.'

This cheered her up.

'Young Biff? Who says so? I think *she*'s another Rosemary or . . . perhaps we should call her Anna?'

Glad that she seemed better, he laughed.

'Why not indeed?'

Immediately, Rosemary wrote a letter back. He read it, relieved to see that there was no mention of his flying duties, or the weather, or, thank God, any mention of Spain other than: yes — meeting next year would be wonderful.

Most of it was about the time they'd had together, reminiscing about silly things like when Konrad had been showing off on a diving board and had fallen in with a huge belly-flop, soaking a passing waiter, or Biff, finding himself surrounded by irate traders when he'd accidentally knocked over a wickerwork tray of lemons that had rolled down the stone-flagged street with amazing speed. She enclosed another photograph, not from the holiday, but from their wedding. It showed only them and their parents, whom she detailed on the back, standing under a large cedar tree with the church beyond.

Biff could hardly see how they could make out that it was in any way a security *leak*.

A week passed. There was great excitement in the squadron as they learned that they were to be re-equipped early in the New Year with the greatly improved and more powerful Mark IV version with the redesigned longer nose.

And still there was no letter from Germany

on the mat in the morning, or the afternoon.

Biff was conscious of the CO looking at him one day, and wondered whether he knew something that he didn't, but nothing was ever said.

She had sent a Christmas Card but 25 December came and went without any word. Biff had to be orderly officer over the holiday period. He waited on the men, serving their Christmas lunch, together with the CO and senior non-commissioned officers. It was a service tradition.

In the end Rosemary, as she sat on the floor one evening before the fire, stockinged toes wriggling as she tried to warm them, her back resting against their chintzy sofa, murmured sadly:

'I think something has happened, don't you? Konrad and Anna, especially Anna, would not have stopped like that. She would have sent a card, I'm sure.'

Biff was reading the paper. Bradman had scored 225 in a match between Queensland and South Australia, and in the England v. South Africa test match Tom Goddard had taken a hat trick and Paul Gibb had scored 93 and 106 on his debut.

He closed the paper, looked at the carriage clock on the mantelpiece. It was nearly nine o'clock.

'Maybe our letters aren't getting through — or theirs to us. The world is very untrusting at the moment.'

They sat in silence, broken only by the hiss and crackle and pop of the fire. Shadows from the flames flickered on the walls. He stirred.

'I'll get the Ovaltine. Would you like the wireless on?'

She nodded, held up her hand for him to touch as he passed.

'Thank you, darling. We'll get the news.'

It was cold in the kitchen. He struck a match, lit the gas ring with a 'plop', put some water in the kettle from the single tap over the deep white sink with the galvanized bucket beneath, and put it over the flame in preparation for their hot-water bottles. He then filled a saucepan with milk from a bottle in the larder. He took two large cups from the brass hooks where they hung under a wall cupboard and spooned in the Ovaltine, then he went back into the warmth of the sitting-room.

The BBC announcer was speaking of the Royal Family, who had attended church again that day; the Princesses Elizabeth and Margaret Rose had been seen waving from the windows of the royal car.

Mr Chamberlain had spent a quiet time at

Chequers. Heavy snow was forecast in Scotland and the North. With that the melodious tones wished them all a peaceful goodnight.

Rosemary suddenly realized he was leaning on the back of the sofa, listening.

'Biff — the milk.'

He heard the hiss of overflowing Jersey on to the flames even as he dodged around the door. The smell of burnt milk filled the kitchen.

He lifted the saucepan — then dropped it, swearing, back on to the stove, the handle was so hot.

He turned off the gas, got the dishcloth and began mopping up, aware that Rosemary had appeared in the doorway.

She clicked her tongue.

'Men. How on earth do you manage to fly an aeroplane?'

He was just glad she didn't seem to be angry.

They attended the New Year's eve party in the mess, but Rosemary was getting more and more tired and sleepy in the evenings. She rested all afternoon in preparation while Biff worked on the car, cleaning the carburettor and foot-pumping the tyres. His hands were frozen, and by the time he'd finished and gone inside he urgently needed a pee. He opened the back door and trotted up the red-bricked path to the outside lavatory.

Inside, his fingers were so numb that he fumbled with his fly buttons, unable to undo them. Vigorously rubbing his hands together he blew hard on the knuckles, stamping his feet not only to help his circulation, but to ward off the imminent need for relief. When he eventually managed it he gritted his teeth with the discomfort.

Rosemary wasn't showing yet, but in the flowing gown she had chosen you would never have known. Biff thought she was radiant. When they entered the mess several heads turned, and 'Dicky' Dickinson took her by the arm.

'Rosemary, you look wonderful.'

'Thank you, Allan,' she used his real name. 'You look pretty good too in your mess kit. Very distinguished.'

He laughed. 'Let me get you a drink.'

'Just an orange squash please.' She indicated her tummy. 'I've gone right off anything interesting.'

More people crowded in, forcing them towards the centre table which was decorated with holly and berries.

Suddenly Biff realized that the CO was standing there, with his wife.

'Biff, good to see you, and Rosemary; you

look absolutely delightful.'

He turned to his wife and attracted her attention.

'My dear, this is Rosemary Banks — Biff's wife — do you remember? You met her at that shindig at Frampton Manor.'

'I do indeed.' The CO's wife was a tall lady, well-connected it was said. She was rather plain, but her eyes were lively.

'You ride to hounds, I believe?'

'Not at the moment. I'm expecting our first child.'

'My dear, I had no idea.'

They talked on as the CO faced Biff.

'How are you enjoying the squadron?'

'Very much, sir.'

'Good, good.'

The CO nodded, took a sip of single malt, seemed to be making up his mind.

'That business of your German friends — all resolved now?'

'Yes sir, we haven't heard from them at all.'

The CO nodded.

'Good, good.' When he realized what he'd said, he carried on hastily: 'I mean — good thing it's not worrying you.'

He looked down, frowning into his drink.

'I was very embarrassed about that visit we had — didn't like it at all.'

He took a gulp of the whisky.

'Always been a flying man — the desk side can be a bit of a bind.'

'I understand, sir.'

As soon as midnight came, with the sound of Big Ben transmitted over the Tannoys from the BBC broadcast, the mess erupted into deafening cheering and the screeching of party trumpets. Suddenly an 'old man' with a long white beard, a scythe, and wearing a tunic with 1938 written on it, ran through the room. He'd got half-way round when he was suddenly divested of his tunic by grasping hands. In his underpants he legged it away down the corridor as 'the baby New Year' came through the front door; a very hairy man in a giant napkin made from towels with massive safety pins. On his hairy chest was written 1939. He was grabbed and hoisted on to somebody's shoulder. Squirting beer from his large feeding-bottle, he was paraded in triumph around the room, ending up in the middle as the crowd sang Auld Lang Syne, roaring up to him before receding and then coming at him again.

Eventually he too, lost his 'decency', only he didn't have anything on underneath. Women screamed, a door was knocked off its hinges, as, hands clasped firmly over his manhood, '1939' disappeared down the corridor pursued by a man cracking his towel at his naked backside.

In January Biff had leave, so they went first to his parents, then on to Rosemary's. A week after they got back the first of the new long-nosed Mark IVs was delivered to the squadron, or rather, to the CO.

The CO spent the afternoon being familiarized with the aircraft, and then showing off his new toy, roaring over the mess and doing climbing turns that demonstrated the increased power and manoeuverability.

He *was* a flying man.

Back on the ground they were all over and in it. When Biff got home, full of excitement, he burst into the cottage.

'Rosemary.'

There was no reply. He called up the small staircase, though he knew she must have heard him if she was there.

'Darling?'

Then he realized that she must be in the lavatory. He opened the back door and called out.

'Rosemary.'

When there was still no reply he walked up the path, knocked on the door. When it remained quiet he tried the latch. The door opened. It was empty.

He began to worry when there was no sign of her an hour later. He was just deciding to go back to the Mess to see if there had been any telephone messages, when a large black Wolseley 14 drew up at the gate. He recognized the man in the Homburg straight away; it was Dr Monks, their, or rather Rosemary's, GP.

He hurried down the path and reached the car as the doctor in his overcoat got out of the door. He was looking very sombre.

'Is everything all right? Is Rosemary with you?'

Doctor Monks took him by the elbow.

'Let's go inside, Mr Banks.'

Heart thumping, Biff led the way into the cottage. The doctor shut the door behind him.

Biff could wait no longer.

'Is it Rosemary? Has she had an accident?'

Doctor Monks shook his head.

'No, she will be all right, I'm sure.'

Biff suddenly realized what was coming.

'It's the baby?'

The doctor grimaced.

'Unfortunately your wife saw some bleeding this morning. She came straight to the surgery. When I examined her I had to break the news that her baby was — I'm very sorry — already dead.'

Biff was stunned, just stood there.

'Apparently Mrs Banks had felt something

wasn't quite right for some two weeks. She already had an appointment when things took their own course.'

With some difficulty Biff finally managed to gather himself together.

'Where is she? Is she in danger?'

Dr Monks tried to reassure him.

'I've come to take you to the cottage hospital. She will be all right. Nature is just having its natural way.'

Biff said: 'Can you wait while I change out of uniform? I'll be very quick.'

The doctor gestured with his hat.

'Of course. And you must pack a small case for your wife — nightdress, underwear, toothbrush, that sort of thing.'

Biff started to unbutton his jacket as he climbed the stairs. All he could think about was poor Rosemary, and what she was going through.

And the baby boy, or girl, he would now never know.

10

It was dark, but he could see the outline of the bed and then, as he turned over, the lights of his bedside clock. It was 3.22 in the morning. He knew what had awakened him, he needed to go to the lavatory. He slowly swung his legs out of bed, until they rested on the carpet. He waited a few moments before hauling himself shakily to his feet. With one hand always supporting himself, first on the bedside cabinet, then the chest of drawers, he managed to reach the *en suite*. Biff didn't switch on the light — from past experience he knew it would make it harder to get back to sleep if he did, it took such a long time these days to pass water.

He could see the toilet seat in the dim light from the window. Dropping his pyjama pants he lowered himself carefully down.

When he'd finished he stood up. The dizziness was instant. He'd stumbled several times the last few weeks without any harm; he hadn't told anybody. But this time his head struck the door post. A blaze of coloured lights filled his vision, then utter complete blackness.

They were going to the cinema to see an eagerly awaited film. It was several weeks after they had lost their little girl. He waited downstairs whilst she finished fixing her face. If truth were told, he was concerned about Rosemary's health, she wasn't her old self. Nothing he could put his finger on really, but — he shook his head at the Royal Doulton spaniel on the mantelpiece — she seemed so remote.

Rosemary came down the stairs into the room.

'Right, I'm ready.'

He was relieved to see she was smartly dressed and made up, it made *him* feel better, at least.

They splashed out and sat in the circle for the princely sum of one-and-ninepence.

The first film was a cowboy, with the hero in a tall white Stetson, everybody riding madly around and firing guns, the discharges seeming to go up into the air, though the baddies and Indians fell off their horses just the same. The posse passed an identical cactus several times, he noted.

In the interval he got themselves tubs of ice cream. When the house lights went down again a bright spotlight picked out a man in a dinner jacket at the keyboard of a large Wurlitzer in the pit. As he played, the whole organ rose steadily up until he was level with the stage.

Ten minutes of a medley of popular songs followed, then he descended again. At the last moment he turned and waved, the light reflecting on his glasses before it was extinguished.

Biff lit a couple of Craven As and passed her one, before the curtains clicked and rolled back. The Gaumont British News followed, the strident voice of the commentator excitedly adding details as smoke from their cigarettes joined that of others to curl up into the flickering lights of the projector.

One item did attract Biff's attention.

On 14 February a German battleship, the *Bismarck*, was launched. The great hull slid into the water of the Elbe at the Blohm & Voss dockyards in Hamburg, dragging huge chains behind it to slow it down. Thousands were watching Herr Hitler launch it, and he wondered if Konrad was there, and perhaps Anna, but he wouldn't say anything to Rosemary — not in her present depressed frame of mind.

At last the film they had been waiting to see came on, *Jezebel*, the story of a headstrong young woman of the old South, played by Bette Davis.

The music swelled.

He reached out his hand and found hers. She didn't take it away, but there was no great response either. Biff's heart sank.

That night he got into bed beside her. Before he could do or say anything she kissed him on the cheek and abruptly turned over, saying: 'Good night. Got an early start in the morning.'

With his light out he turned on his side, away from her, staring at the tiny cottage window with its four little panes, and the twinkling stars beyond.

He knew by the sound of her breathing, even if he couldn't see her open eyes, that she was not asleep.

Some days the despair was almost too much to bear. He'd not only lost a child, but a wife as well.

Fortunately for him, in the following weeks the pace of training increased and the squadron spent many hours perfecting bombing techniques on barges moored in the estuary nearby.

The arrival of the Mark IV variant in large numbers perked up everybody's spirits. With its twin 840-horsepower engines it was capable of carrying two 500lb armour-piercing bombs at a speed comparable to that of many fighters. It could range deep into an enemy's territory, and a ventral pack of four machineguns, with another gun on the wing, and a semi-retractable dorsal turret, meant it had plenty of firepower.

The only things that seemed to help Rosemary were horse-riding and tennis. The riding she managed by getting up, very early in the morning, before he did, and then going straight on to work; the tennis she played at weekends. He was aware that she seemed not to want to be with him for any length of time.

Nearly six months after Munich Nazi troops occupied what remained of Czechoslovakia, and in the mess there was a growing feeling that war with Germany was now almost inevitable. Biff could only think of Konrad and Anna. In his loneliness of the last month or so he'd often thought of that brilliantly happy October, when Rosemary and Anna had laughed so much. Now Rosemary seemed almost a different person.

One night, after she had gone to bed, he sat before the fire and listened to the BBC. The Prime Minister had written personally to the Poles on 31 March, telling them that if their independence was ever threatened *His Majesty's Government and the French Government would at once lend them all the support in their power.*

So that was that. If Herr Hitler ever invaded Poland, war would follow.

At least now they knew where they stood.

On 7 April Mussolini invaded Albania.

Biff, ten days later, with *The Times* opened before him, was sitting in a leather easy chair in the mess with a cup of coffee beside him, served by one of the white-coated mess servants. He read that Britain, France, and *Russia*, of all places, given the antipathy the Government felt towards the Communist state, had signed an anti-Nazi pact.

His worries over Rosemary and where they were going was, with almost every passing day, being overshadowed by a terrible sense of inevitability, a drift to a nightmare future that would engulf them and their cosy little life, with all its problems. But an awareness of what might be coming didn't make the prospect seem any the less threatening.

They managed somehow to get through the next couple of months, but in June, Biff came home early one day to find Rosemary in the garden, using a watering can, and *singing* gently to herself.

Hesitantly he said: 'Hello, darling. Had a good day?'

She smiled at him, a warmth in her eyes that he hadn't seen for a very long time.

'Yes, I have.'

Rosemary put the can down carefully, turned, paused, and then gave him a hug. She stood back, looking sad, and anxiously searched his face.

'I know I've been away, Biff, but I'm back now, I promise. Can you ever forgive me?'

He found he could hardly breathe, fearful that he hadn't heard her properly. Hadn't understood what seemed to be happening — a miracle.

He swallowed. 'There is nothing to forgive, darling.'

They just stood there, holding on. The coldness and depression had lifted as swiftly as a morning fog in a rising sun.

Rosemary couldn't explain it, any more than Biff could believe it. But his heart sang.

★ ★ ★

'Jeeze, skipper, what's got into you?'

The bomber/navigator turned around, looking at him wild-eyed.

Biff grinned. He'd just brought the Blenheim light bomber in at less than 200 feet, over the sea, over the dunes, and on across the airfield, flying like a demented Biggles. They were on the local air defence exercises and it had become glaringly obvious that despite all their expectations and beliefs

189

the new generation of single-seat interceptor fighters, the Hawker Hurricane, had run rings around them. Biff, still feeling on top of the world, had twisted and dived from cloud to cloud and then gone right down on to the deck to get back to 'bomb' his airfield.

He was one of only five aircraft out of twenty-three to do so.

Afterwards there was much discussion in the mess and a lot of accusations made against the 'fighter boys' for over-exaggeration. Most of the squadron still insisted that the bomber — especially the fast and elusive Blenheim — would always get through. The big test would come in the August national RAF defence exercises: these would confirm it one way or the other. When the final debriefing was done he jumped into his new Singer 9 sports car and headed for home. Tonight they were going to a dinner-dance at the George Hotel in town.

He reached home, skidding on the gravel and jumping out without opening the little door, to find that Rosemary was upstairs, still in her satin pink petticoat, fixing her earrings.

He burst into the bedroom, pulling off his already undone tunic and flinging it on to a chair, upon which he promptly sat and started on his shoes.

'Sorry, darling, they kept us waiting around

while they evaluated the results. Bloody waste of time.'

He threw his shoes across the room and slipped his braces off his shoulders, unbuttoning his flies and getting out of his blue-serge trousers as fast as he could.

It was only then that he realized that Rosemary hadn't said as much as a word, and was standing by her dressing-table, hand on her hip.

For a brief, awful moment he thought she had had a relapse; then he saw what she had in her other hand, and the twinkle in her eye. She had got it from a box in his bedside cabinet. He always bought them every time he visited his barber.

Biff could hardly restrain himself, crossing to her, picking her up with both hands cupping her bottom as she wrapped her strong legs around his waist, arms about his neck, kissing fiercely. He carried her to the bed, collapsing on top of her, running his hands up her thigh.

She was wearing no knickers, laughing at the look on his face as he suddenly found out.

Rosemary had already opened the little square packet. She pulled down his shorts, helped with one hand by Biff, then she deftly rolled the french letter on to him.

At that moment she lost control as Biff, a

ravenous hunger for his lovely, beautiful wife — denied to him for so long — at last got the better of him.

He pinned her arms to the pillow above her head with one hand, as with the other he bared her breasts and ran his fingers over the hardening nipples.

Then he penetrated her with ease; Rosemary's body was more than ready for him.

For several minutes they rucked with increasing fury until at last, with explosion after explosion in his head and loins, he collapsed beside her.

They lay side by side gasping for air. Several minutes passed before Rosemary managed to whisper:

'I'm so sorry, darling, I'm so sorry.'

He pulled her on to her side as he rolled to face her, and took her in his arms, gently kissing her all over her face, lifting a strand of blonde hair out of her eyes and hugging her very gently.

'Stop darling, stop. You're back now — that's all that matters.'

★ ★ ★

Throughout June and July they played tennis, went to the local 'rep' to see plays, and saw a succession of wonderful films: *Goodbye Mr Chips* with Robert Donat, *Wuthering Heights* with Olivier and the stunningly beautiful Merle Oberon, and *Dark Victory* with Bette Davis.

On the newsreels the King and Queen visited America, the first reigning monarchs to do so since the revolution. Later, on another occasion, they saw the Princess Elizabeth, now a young woman, meeting Royal Navy officers including a handsome young prince of the Greek royal family.

They got tickets for Wimbledon, eating strawberries and cream with lots of sugar, before watching the ladies final as Alice Marble beat Kay Stammers 6-2, 6-0, and raised the silver Rosewater Dish in front of her.

On the same day they watched one of the rounds of the mixed doubles. When it was over Rosemary said wistfully: 'Konrad and Anna would have loved that.'

Biff didn't reply, just nodded.

So, she still thought of them, as he had many a time, especially when she had been so depressed.

The first of August found them on holiday in Cornwall. They'd rented a fisherman's cottage for a week, in Port Isaac. Hand in hand they climbed the steep streets and then the lanes and, at the last, a dirt path, toiling in the sun, listening to the bees busy on the flowers and gorse, until they reached the top of the headland, and the full breeze of the green-blue Atlantic cooled their fevered brows.

Following the rocky coast the path dipped into a steep fern-covered combe. Water bubbled down the hillside, sparkling in the sun, before running on, cold and clear over the stones in the deep shade.

'Here — this is the place.'

Rosemary pointed at a flat sheltered area of short grass flanked by rocks and the edge of the stream, and surrounded by ferns. Further back, a dense clump of short trees, deformed by the ceaseless wind, formed an almost impenetrable screen.

Black-and-white cows grazed the small fields above.

Biff pulled the strap of his haversack off one shoulder and swung it to the ground.

Rosemary had a large bag. From it she took a tartan blanket and spread it carefully out on the grass. Biff delivered their thermos and various tins.

The scratched red Oxo box contained their sandwiches; another, little jellies she'd made the night before. From her bag Rosemary set out two glasses and a bottle of Tizer. Lastly,

Biff placed the portable gramophone, which he'd carried separately, on a flat piece of rock.

He sat down cross-legged.

'I'm famished.'

Rosemary settled herself with her legs to one side, and handed him a linen napkin.

'Really, Biff, after that huge breakfast — you'll be getting fat.'

She pushed at the metal device attached to the stopper on the Tizer bottle. With a hiss the stopper opened and the fizzing reddish liquid welled up out of the neck. She poured two tumblerfuls and handed him one.

'Here, quench your thirst.'

He did as he was told as she opened the Oxo tin. Inside, wrapped in greaseproof paper, were the egg sandwiches she'd made that morning.

Rosemary offered them; Biff took one.

Before she could take one herself he'd wolfed it down.

'That's good.'

Rosemary tut-tutted. 'For heaven's sake, Biff.'

They ate their way steadily through all the sandwiches, jellies and cakes, finishing with coffee and some *petits fours*.

'I'm stuffed.'

Biff lay flat, legs bent at the knee, arms behind his head, staring straight up into a blue sky with fluffy white clouds racing by, listening to unseen skylarks.

Leisurely, Rosemary packed everything away, leaving only the blanket on which they sat, and turned her attention to the portable gramophone. She selected a favourite record, put it on to the turntable, then cranked the winder until it would go no more. With a click the black wax disc started turning. Rosemary raised the arm, and brought the needle down on the undulating surface. She flopped down beside Biff, her head resting on his arm as the first notes of 'Smoke Gets in your Eyes' rose into the air.

She snuggled into him.

'Hmm, this is heaven on earth.'

He gave her a squeeze and closed his eyes. When the plaintive song ended, Rosemary murmured: 'In a few weeks it will be the first of October. We should have been meeting Anna and Konrad.'

He nodded. 'I know, darling.'

11

A vicious pain was sliding down his neck and arm. It was pitchblack.

There seemed to be no glimmer of light anywhere. Where was he? What had happened? He couldn't remember. The pain was awful, like an iron band around his chest. In a cold sweat Biff lay looking up into the blackness. He wondered about pressing the alarm thing around his neck, but then, mercifully, he lost consciousness again.

★   ★   ★

As they walked back, there was a deep roar of several aircraft engines. Biff searched the sky but there was nothing to see.

'Must have been the other side of the hill, they sounded very low down.'

It was the RAF's big August exercise. He wondered how the squadron was faring.

On their last day they drove through the winding high-banked lanes to St Ives, famous for its artists. Barbara Hepworth a sculptor was busy in her workshop, according to a man who was addressing a little group outside the house. Suddenly the door opened and the woman herself invited them inside. Biff grabbed Rosemary's arm and towed her in as if they were part of the group.

Afterwards he asked had she enjoyed it?

'Oh yes,' she said, 'but I can't really say I understood those shapes.'

They went to the harbour and looked at the fishing boats with their bright red and blue hulls lying high and dry on the sand at low tide.

A naval high-speed patrol boat was anchored out in deep water.

On a table outside a little shop they enjoyed scones with cream and jam, and a pot of tea, watching people drift past, some wearing Kiss Me Quick hats, some eating ice creams, and candy floss.

A Salvation Army band came marching along with a little crowd following behind, and children running alongside. They stopped, and an officer got on a box and spoke to the crowd. The band then played one of the Olney hymns: 'Amazing Grace'. A collection was taken, before they marched off to 'Onward, Christian Soldiers'.

He looked at his watch. 'We'd better get a move on.'

It marked the end of their holiday.

Next day, on the long journey home, the

car boiled up in Bridgwater. After letting it cool Biff refilled the radiator with a kettle of water provided by a woman outside whose house they'd stopped.

She also looked around and found several bottles which she filled with more water for the journey.

It was a good thing she did. They boiled up again outside Taunton, and although he was not a member, a passing AA man on his yellow motorbike and sidecar, helped with water from a large can he was carrying.

Finally, just short of Bristol, Biff had to replace the splitting water hose, which meant walking a mile to the nearest garage as Rosemary read a book. The garage man brought him back in his Ford truck.

It took him another half an hour to replace the hose, fill the system up from a can provided by the garage, and bleed out the bubbles.

Midnight came and went before the pale yellow of his headlights lit up the cottage. Rosemary was fast asleep. When he gently aroused her she groaned and rubbed her neck.

'I'm so stiff.'

Biff got the key in the door while the headlights lit up the front of the house.

By the time they got into bed it was two

o'clock in the morning.

He had to report to the squadron at seven.

The rest of August passed quickly enough. He was just home, getting ready to go to the tennis club for an evening of 'friendlies' and supper when the wireless broadcast the early evening bulletin for 27 August. He could hear it from downstairs. Herr Hitler was demanding Danzig and the Polish corridor.

Biff froze, sagged down on to the bed listening, his trousers around his knees, a sinking feeling in his stomach. He knew that the end was near now: the end of peace.

There was a subdued atmosphere at the club that night, none of the alcohol-fuelled wildness of the partying that had gone on in some quarters of society all summer.

Three days later Poland mobilized.

A white-faced Rosemary turned from what she was doing in the kitchen when he walked in.

'What's the word on the squadron?'

He shook his head. 'We're in the dark as much as everybody else.'

They had their usual glass of sherry, while in the oven a steak-and-kidney pie bubbled and dribbled out of the airhole in the pastry and down the sides of the dish.

'What do you think is going to happen, Biff?'

He took a deep breath.

'It's serious Rose, but who knows? Mr Chamberlain may pull something out of the bag again?'

When they made love that night it was with a quiet intensity.

Afterwards they remained close together, just hanging on to each other, not wanting to be physically parted.

Next day Germany was reporting a Polish attack on one of their radio stations in Gleiwitz.

It seemed so unlikely as to defy reason.

On 1 September German armies crossed into Poland.

Britain and France issued demands that they must be withdrawn.

Two days later Neville Chamberlain addressed the nation, his tired, defeated voice ending with: 'and consequently this country is at war with Germany.'

It was a Sunday, but Biff drove immediately to the airfield and was told to go away, come in as normal on the Monday. So he returned to a worried Rosemary and did some frenzied digging in the vegetable patch. Later, as was their custom, they went to the tennis club. The courts were closed, the nets taken down and already packed away. The mood in the clubhouse was subdued. There were no displays of patriotism such as their parents had shared a generation before, Passchendaele and the Somme had seen to that. But there was a quiet air of resigned determination that their cause was righteous.

Rosemary turned to him, obviously with something important to say, but finding it difficult.

Anxiously he asked: 'What is it, darling?'

She swallowed and for the first time he realized that she had tears in her eyes.

'This means that you and Konrad are enemies now, doesn't it?'

He shook his head. 'We'll never be enemies, Rosemary.'

But sadly, he knew they were — technically.

The Blenheims were first in action, though Biff was not one of their pilots.

Ten aircraft had attacked German warships in the Heligoland Bight, but had failed to achieve any real damage.

Worst of all, the losses were terrible. Half of them failed to return.

They'd all been affected. From his wedding guard of honour Allan 'Dicky' Dickinson and three others were not at their places that night.

The war was less than a week old, and already one of the most decent of men, a true

Yorkshire man and salt of the earth, was gone. It was difficult to believe that he would never hear his gritty 'bugger off', said with a certain twinkle in the eye; never again have the benefit of his earthy wit and wisdom, his pithy comments on Biff's performance at Rugby.

The morale of the squadron had taken a big knock.

Biff felt a mixture of guilt and frustration. He'd trained all these years, wanted to prove himself, and had felt it keenly when his aircraft had been pronounced unserviceable just as they were to be briefed.

But he was still alive.

Rosemary, when he was allowed off station, flew into his arms as he stepped out of the car. After they'd made love they lay side by side, holding hands. Rosemary let go and found her cigarettes, offered them, but Biff shook his head.

She lit up, then lay back, exhaling smoke, watching it drift up towards the ceiling.

'God, I needed that. I'm smoking more than ever now, worrying about you, where you are, what you are doing. Every time a Blenheim goes over I get jittery.'

He squeezed her hand.

'Don't be. All I've done are some anti-shipping patrols.'

He didn't say anything to her about the enormous fear of imminent attack when he was in the air. When he'd got back from the first patrol his back ached, his neck ached, and he had a headache from straining to see tiny dots falling out of the sun on to him — enemy fighters. It got better as the weeks passed, his fear was still there, but was now confined to somewhere at the back of his mind, though his eyes still ceaselessly roamed the sky for danger.

'I've got a forty-eight. What would you like to do?'

She turned her head, smiled.

'Stay here and make love, morning, noon and night.'

Biff still remembered that terrible time of a few months ago.

'Very well, madam, be it on your own head.'

With that he rolled on to her, Rosemary screaming: 'Watch my ciggy! Biff — Biff!'

★   ★   ★

The German army took until 4 October to subdue the last remnants of Polish resistance and annex Western Poland, the Russians taking the Eastern half in the unholy alliance that had been the secret Soviet-German

Treaty. Everybody in the Air Force, and most civilians too, had noted the firebombing of Warsaw by the Luftwaffe.

On 5 October Adolf Hitler denied he wanted war with Britain. The only action so far had been by U-boats, sinking the liner *Athenia* soon after war was declared. One air-raid had occurred, but everywhere else was all quiet.

The British Expeditionary Force was now well deployed in France, as the happy scenes at the cinema of grinning, gap-toothed Tommies in French villages with young girls on their arms demonstrated. The newsreel ended with a stirring commentary to the effect that if Hitler made a move on France, these were the chaps to give him a bloody nose.

Rosemary finished her ice cream and put the tub under the seat. She had been looking forward to the big film, and didn't want to know anything more about the war for now, thank you very much.

As the opening scenes of *Ninotchka* with Greta Garbo flickered on the screen, she leant against her husband, content and happy for at least another twelve hours.

With the turn of a screw though, the war did become more brutal the following week when a U-boat got into Scapa Flow and sunk the battleship HMS *Royal Oak*, with 833 sailors drowned.

Life went on as usual, Biff flying his anti-shipping patrols, Rosemary still working in her estate agents, though it got very slow. She did enrol in the Women's Voluntary Service, and manned a mobile canteen on half-closing day, taking it to railway and bus stations in the area.

There was excitement in December when three Royal Navy cruisers cornered the pocket battleship *Graf Spee* at the battle of the River Plate, forcing it to take shelter in Montevideo harbour. Four days later the Germans scuttled her.

Everybody hailed the great victory, but Biff and Rosemary did wonder about Konrad. Could he have been on the ship? If so, was he alive and well, though interned, not able to see Anna for probably a couple of years.

If it were true, Rosemary would be envious, worrying as she did every day about Biff. But she would be pleased for Anna.

They were together for Christmas, paying flying visits to both sets of parents, travelling by dirty, heavily overloaded trains.

On the day itself they were on their own, roasting a locally provided goose before settling before a log fire, listening to the King's speech from the floor, where they were cracking nuts that she had bought before the war, drinking sherry and Watney's brown ale, and getting through a whole box of chocolates that her mother had given them as a present.

He had already told her that he wouldn't be with her for New Year's Eve; the squadron had been ordered to France to join the air component of the BEF and the Advanced Air Striking Force. She had accepted it resignedly. Even without any fighting the war had already taken over their lives. Nothing would ever be the same, she thought, even if it all went away tomorrow. They'd already lost some of the innocence of their youth. Maybe, of course, it was just that they would have changed anyway: they were getting used to being married, after all.

On Christmas night they listened to the wireless, until the wet batteries ran out. Fortunately they had stand-by ones for the holiday period, under the sink in the kitchen, but he couldn't be bothered to change them until the morning. It was freezing cold in the bedroom. They flung their clothes off and dived under the covers, holding on, teeth chattering, until the combined heat of their entwined bodies turned the 'tent' they were in into a little hothouse. For the first time they lay in union side by side, Biff staying in her until it just naturally withdrew after a long time.

Later, he got into trouble for breaking

wind, especially as he forced her to stay under the sheets.

When she eventually surfaced, gasping and flailing her arms, he leapt out and stark naked flew downstairs, and out of the back door to the lavatory, feeling the cold creeping into his bones as he stood there, pulling the chain and running back in again — except that Rosemary had locked the back door.

He banged and shouted:

'Let me in. Rosemary, let me in — I'm dying of cold. Let me in.'

Her voice came from the other side.

'Say you're sorry — and that you will never do that again.'

He held his hands to his rapidly freezing — and shrinking — manhood.

'I promise. I'll never do it again.'

He stamped his bare feet.

'Hurry up, please.'

Rosemary's voice came through the wood and glass again.

'You haven't said sorry.'

'I'm sorry.' He pleaded. 'Rosemary, if you don't open the door soon I'll freeze to death. You don't want that, do you?'

'Hmm. If you ever do that childish, boys' boarding house thing again, I will leave you out there. Now, say sorry again.'

'Sorry — sorry — sorry.'

As soon as he heard the bolt slide back he pushed at the door. With a squeak Rosemary fled up the stairs.

'Now you behave, Biff. It's only what you deserved.'

He caught her by the bed, sat down and turned her over his knee, gave a few hearty slaps to the bouncing bare bottom, before spinning her round and giving her a kiss as she sat on his lap.

'Now, warm me up, wife.'

They went back into bed, shivering again until warmth brought sleep.

The day came when he had to return to the squadron. She used the flatiron heated on the hob in the kitchen to press some of his shirts, and pack his brown suitcases.

He carried them out to the car, putting one on the back seat and one on the front, on its end.

He was dressed in his blue RAF greatcoat, which had become heavy in the drizzle that now fell.

'Well, that's it, darling. I'd better be off.'

Rosemary looked as miserable as he felt at leaving her. Back in the kitchen he took off his cap.

'Don't come out again — I'll be gone in a flash.'

She was in her white mackintosh, a scarf

around her head, its ends passed under her chin and tied at the back. He put his large hands on both sides of her head, and searched her face as she looked back at him. There was nothing further to be said. She had already exhorted him many times to be careful, not to do anything foolish.

He knew he had to go quickly. He kissed her gently.

'I'll be back soon enough, darling.'

'You promise to write — every day?'

He nodded. 'Every day.'

Biff couldn't resist another kiss, then turned, bumping clumsily into the door before crunching across the gravel to the car. As he opened its door he turned. Rosemary was in the doorway. He gave a nod, which she acknowledged, then he squeezed his frame into the tight space behind the wheel and slammed the forward-opening door.

The engine burst into noisy, growling life.

In too much of a hurry, eager to cut short the agony, he managed to crash the gears. He eventually got it into first, dropped the handbrake and turned out of the gate.

He gave a quick wave, but the figure in the doorway didn't move.

He felt a lump in his throat.

12

They crossed the channel, flying in formation with another squadron; the view of so many Blenheims was an uplifting sight. After all the anti-shipping and reconnaissance patrols, and the 'nickelling' (the dropping of propaganda leaflets), at last they were going as a bomber force in strength.

Biff brought his aircraft down on a grass strip near the Belgian border, and taxied to dispersal. Immediately ground crews scrambled all over the Blenheim. The air of frenzied activity made the blood tingle. Fuel bowsers and Hillman crew-cars criss-crossed the field; groups of 'erks' arrived in endless convoys of three-tonners with spares and ammunition, and were already unloading the supplies into tents scattered, like the aircraft, under the cover of trees.

Their mess was a handsome château, with a formal garden and an elegant eighteenth-century dining-room.

What would he not have given to hear Dickie's comments on their splendid billet?

He immediately set pen to paper, writing to Rosemary. Although he couldn't give any details of their position — the censors would see to that — he did manage to give her the flavour of the rather grand life he was enjoying.

On his first day, with an excited navigator who doubled as wireless operator and bomb-aimer, and the dorsal gunner, they were ordered to patrol the Luxembourg border. Three pairs of eyes combed the skies and the ground for the enemy, but there was nothing to see.

Surveillance soon settled in a routine, the only convoys and troop movements noted being the BEF or the French on the move.

As January gave way to February a severe period of winter weather put paid to many of their operations.

With nothing happening, the euphoria they'd felt on their arrival began to wane, and the château proved to be an icy palace that was unable to keep any heat. The cooks did a terrific job, he wrote to Rosemary by candlelight, the power having gone off again. Their tented field kitchens in the ornamental gardens turned out decent food, and plenty of it, despite the freezing cold. And everywhere the pipes were solid ice.

At last the arctic weather relinquished its iron grip as they moved into March. Rosemary had spent the majority of the nights in the frozen cottage, going to bed wearing slacks, jumper and a woollen hat and, for a couple of days, her overcoat as well. In the beginning, every time she saw the postman crunching up the path between the piles of snow she had shovelled aside her heart went into her mouth, her first thought being; was it a war office telegram being delivered by the regular postman because of the bad conditions?

But as the weeks passed she grew calmer, reading his letters over and over again, going to sleep at night after rereading the latest one under the blankets by torchlight, kissing the place where his crosses indicated he'd pressed his lips to the paper.

And she began to question her own role in the war. She wondered whether to tell him in her next letter, but kept putting it off, not wanting to give him any concern.

★ ★ ★

Biff and a couple of others, stood down for three days, hitched a ride in a transport plane to Paris.

They mingled on the cobbled streets with men in the uniforms of many countries, but overwhelmingly of course the French army and air force.

As they sat outside a café on the Avenue des Champs Elysées near to the Arc de Triomphe, enjoying the first warmish sunlight of the year, passing Parisians gave them welcoming waves.

Biff went to the Louvre, but found most of the exhibits were missing, sent to safer places under the fear of the bomber fleets that might be unleashed on the civilian population, as had happened in Spain. That evening he felt a bit guilty, sitting with his chums, bottles of wine on their table as chorus girls kicked up their long legs and showed them their frilly knickers in a rendition of the cancan: guilty because it seemed that he was deceiving Rosemary, who believed he was suffering on a makeshift airfield facing the German threat, and because it seemed wrong to be excited by the sight of the dancers' bodies.

He was missing her in more ways than one.

All too soon, though, they were back 'home', where the leaves on the trees were beginning to show, the strip becoming greener as the grass began to grow through the surface that was now like a quagmire after being harder than reinforced concrete.

And the tempo of life increased, as news came through at dawn on 9 April that a German invasion fleet had launched an attack on Norway. Denmark was occupied in hours.

The adjutant had broken the news, limping into the mess leaning heavily on his walking stick.

'Well chaps, the balloon's gone up.'

They followed the fortunes of the air force, and particularly the Blenheims, deployed from Britain in the defence of Norway; but with round trips of over 1,000 miles over the sea, it was always going to be too little, too late. Blenheim operations over that country ceased on 2 May.

At sunset Biff stood in a doorway of the mess that night, smoking a cigarette and feeling strangely detached from his body, as though he was observing everything around him from some other vantage point. He knew why. He guessed, like everybody else, that their turn was coming, and some part of him wanted to remember this peaceful corner of France before it was gone for ever.

★ ★ ★

He came round, the pain in his head and arm making him call out in agony. And he was cold, so cold. His hand was resting on the alarm device around his neck. Had he pressed it? He couldn't remember but his fingers wouldn't move as he tried to do so. Was he wounded? He'd been hit as they . . . as they . . . Confused, he couldn't remember. Still frowning, he lost consciousness again.

★ ★ ★

It happened with unbelievable, frightening speed, the whole period lasting less than a month.

On 10 May, at breakfast, they were told that German forces had started to attack the Netherlands, Belgium and Luxembourg and that the famous Maginot Line had been outflanked by an airborne assault.

They scrambled immediately and under the direction of the headquarters of the Advanced Air Striking Force, they were ordered to bomb airfields, bridges and troop columns to stem the invasion.

As they drove out to the dispersed Blenheims they exchanged cheery exhortations to take care, glad at last to be doing something.

He lined up behind the CO, watching as he booted his engines and roared down the runway. In turn Biff moved forward, turned into the wind.

As the skipper's plane came unstuck from mother earth and clawed up into the sky he pushed the two Bristol engines to full power and started rolling.

They were on their way: target, German transport aircraft on the ground in Holland.

There were twelve Blenheims in all. As they passed over the rolling French countryside they could see signs of battle off to the right, and the roads appeared to be jammed with huge columns of people and lorries.

The German-occupied airfield was nearly deserted when they arrived over it. They laid their four 250-pound bombs near some buildings and a Junker 88, watching with satisfaction as explosions and black smoke rose into the air behind them. They were turning for home when about fifty Messerschmitt 109 fighters appeared from the north-east. What followed was carnage. Sweating and terrorstruck, Biff managed to find cloud cover, but saw at least four Blenheims explode or crash in flames. When they got back, only six others landed at varying intervals.

There was no time to agonize over the losses. They were ordered up again — to attack a bridge across which German armour was passing, pursuing the retreating BEF.

Joined by aircraft from another squadron, sixteen in all, they headed for the target. Eight Hurricane fighters rendezvoused with them after ten minutes.

Suddenly the fighter pilots saw the sky fill

with German Me 109s–120 in all.

Despite the fearful odds the Hurricanes turned into the attack as the Blenheims clung to the deck, heading for the target just visible in the distance. Biff heard the gunner shout something over the R/T, and his gun fired, vibrating the aircraft. The bomb-aimer climbed into the nose and readied the bombs.

The first Blenheims ahead of him were now attacking the bridge. He saw the lead aircraft release its bombs, hitting one end of the structure. As the aircraft flew over the bridge at barely one hundred feet it was hit by flak and fell a blazing torch into the riverbank, where it exploded.

Biff was concentrating on keeping a steady line for the bomb-aimer's benefit, but he could see in his mirror a Messerschmitt looming up behind. His gunner was blazing away but the enemy opened up with his cannons. As Biff watched he saw the turret hit. It splintered as his crewman collapsed in a welter of blood. He would be next.

'Bombs away.'

In that split second he yanked the yoke and tramped the rudder bar, putting the plane almost on its side, engines screaming as he crossed over one of the bridge towers. The sky was a mass of tracer streamers and black puffs of shellbursts. He didn't see or know how it happened, but the Jerry was no longer with him, instead was carrying straight on with smoke trailing behind him. Miraculously Biff had escaped the flak that had hit their own fighter.

Chest thumping, sweat pouring down his face, getting in his eyes, his pants wet with urine, he hedge-hopped for home.

Back on the ground the medics got his turret gunner out — dead — and covered his body with a tarpaulin. Intelligence reported the bridge still standing. Six aircraft failed to return.

As night fell he slumped in the mess, staring unseen at the food. There was masses of it, more than half the chairs were empty at the dining-table.

A few days later it was obvious that the Allied ground and air forces were facing total defeat. Twice they had to abandon their airfield hastily and fly further back. The German advance was relentless: nothing or nobody seemed able to stop it. Everywhere they met resistance they used their Stuka dive-bombers, the menacing gull-winged birds of prey filling the air with their frightening banshee wail as they dived on to their targets. Towering columns of black smoke rising in the air marked the end of resistance. Huge columns of refugees jammed the roads, so that their ground crews were not waiting for them when they got to the latest, hurriedly marked-out strip. Two days passed before they got fuel and rearmed, for what turned out to be one last attempt to stop the invincible German motorized columns.

The Commander of the AASF gambled everything, putting every available aircraft into the air to bomb the Germans at Sedan.

Nine squadrons, or what was left of them, attacked, including Biff's remaining Blenheims and Fairey Battles.

It was a massacre. Of the seventy-one aircraft that had tried to destroy the pontoon bridges which were the target, only thirty-three returned. The number of crew members who were killed, wounded or taken prisoner was 102, a terrible price as the pontoons remained intact.

Biff got back on one engine, the other had been hit and had caught fire. He'd feathered and extinguished the flames. Half of his plexiglass nose cone was missing, the cockpit was full of blasting cold air. When they'd landed, and he opened the hatch, he'd collapsed on to the wet earth totally exhausted. The ground crew gathered around, looking at the blackened engine and at the fuselage with at least thirty pockmarks from cannon fire.

Only five serviceable aircraft were available

for the next day's operation: another, last attempt, on that damned pontoon bridge. It was ineffectual and only three aircraft returned. Biff wasn't involved. He was watching the CO approach with his wheels down when a desperate shout went up: 'One-o-nines'.

The Messerschmitts came in low with the sun behind them, spraying the field with cannonfire even as Biff dived into a slit trench with two others jumping in on top of him. The CO's plane nosed into the ground and exploded in a ball of flame.

He couldn't see but he heard the explosions as all their remaining aircraft, including his which had been unserviceable, blew up in flames and billowing smoke. The Me 109s also raked anything else they could see, totally unopposed; there were no fighters, no ack-ack, only a few brave souls with 303 rifles, which were completely ineffectual. Several three-tonners went up, and the cooks' tent was hit, killing all three men as they worked to make an evening meal for the survivors.

When it was over, and the other two had got off him he stood up and surveyed the scene. Pillars of black oily smoke rose everywhere he looked.

They had been effectively wiped out. It was

no surprise to Biff when he heard later that no higher loss in operations of a similar size had ever been suffered by the Royal Air Force.

They started the long march to the coast that night — the safest time, along with about a million other people. The roads and lanes were jammed with humanity pushing prams loaded with their worldly goods, white-faced children walking beside them, old folk riding on mattresses piled on lorries. Vehicles of the French and British armies, bicycles, donkeys, cars and carts formed the motley procession to the coast.

As soon as the day dawned, so came the diving Stukas with their devilish screams, and fighters, racing straight up the roads, machine-gunning and ripping to shreds those people caught out before they could jump into ditches or flee into the woods and fields. The roaring exploding flames and billowing acrid smoke, the mangled bodies of man and beast, the screaming and crying, failed to stop the columns forming again, with the relentless pressing need to get away, like animals on the move in Africa.

Tired, hungry and dishevelled, Biff and the remains of the squadron were guided to a place called Dunkirk.

When they got there they had to wait,

sheltering in the sand dunes as enemy aircraft bombed and strafed at will.

Biff looked up, his face covered in wet sand, to see a destroyer standing off shore, hit by a bomb that went straight down one of its three funnels.

The whole ship lifted almost out of the water as it exploded, then fell back into the sea, a flaming hulk.

Nobody could have got out of that.

Great columns of men, like ants, were queuing in orderly rows to the beach edge, then wading out to smaller craft that ferried them out to the bigger ships.

He got away on his third day, 31 May, sitting on the deck of a paddle steamer with a hundred others as they passed the mast of the destroyer still sticking up out of the water, like a giant cross, stark monument to the graves of the men below. He landed at Folkestone in the early hours of the morning, was given a mug of scalding-hot, sweet tea, and a huge wedge of a sandwich, then he was pushed on to a train, lying on the dirty floor, propped against the wall of the lavatory which was in constant use. Heavy boots were clomping around him, and sometimes on him, but he slept so deeply that he had to be shaken roughly to wake him up at Waterloo.

He ended up at a transit camp at Mill Hill,

where he was issued with a shaving-kit, toothbrush and paste, and new underwear and uniform. Stinking as he was, the first thing he wanted to do was get word to Rosemary that he was all right. He went to the office, frantic with people coming and going and telephones ringing. He picked one up and got the operator.

'Hey, you can't use that.'

A young flying officer had come along with a sheaf of papers.

Biff just looked at him. The man saw the expression, the almost dead eyes, the broad shoulders. He faltered. 'Well — be quick about it.'

* * *

Rosemary had been worried sick. His letters had abruptly stopped, and the daily news was confusing, increasingly unbelievable and dreadful. She'd telephoned the squadron office, but nobody could or would give her any information. She apologized to the estate agent, but said she had to stay at home in case . . . in case there was any *news*. They understood. There was hardly any business anyway, except for an increase in homes for rent. So she sat at home, her heart jumping into her mouth every time she saw the postman, or anybody coming along the lane on a bicycle who could be a telegram boy.

So it was a fright when a man she didn't recognize got off his bicycle, undid his trouser clips and walked up the gravel. He wasn't a postman — unless he was an official, come because nobody else wanted to deliver the news.

Feverishly she opened the door, advanced towards him, hardly able to breathe.

The man touched the brim of his trilby.

'Mrs Banks?'

'Yes.'

'I've got some very good news for you.'

Had she heard him properly?

Like an idiot she repeated: 'Good news?'

'Yes. Your husband is safe. He is in a transit camp in London, and will get a letter to you as soon as he can.'

At last it dawned on her.

'Oh!' She threw her arms around him and kissed him soundly on the cheek as the man held on to his hat.

'Thank you,' she said, 'thank you.'

He smiled.

'My pleasure, my dear.'

It was then she said: 'Mr . . . ?'

'Shelton.' He touched his brim again. 'I'm the manager of the shoe shop in the High Street.'

Apparently Biff had phoned her estate

agent office. They had been unable to do anything, but a bit of judicious asking among the other shop owners had produced Mr Shelton, who was only too happy to oblige.

She invited him in for a cup of tea, but he declined — he was on his way home to see his own son, who was due home on embarkation leave before he went to the Far East. He smiled and tapped his nose with a finger and winked as he added: 'Or so I believe.'

So she sat alone in the kitchen, then suddenly rushed up the garden to the lavatory, and brought up all the food she had forced herself to eat for breakfast.

But it didn't matter.

Two days later she waited at the station for him. He had been given a week's leave. The lines began to hum, and then a dark shape with wisps of white steam came round the bend in the distance, gradually getting bigger, the red buffer beam clearly seen.

At last, with a rumble that shook the platform, and with the clanking of its wheels and coupling-rods, the locomotive slowed past her and with a scream of metal on metal braked to a halt in a surge of steam.

Crowds got off, a porter pulled a trolley past with galvanized milk churns on it. She couldn't see him. Then, out of the clouds of steam rising up from beneath a carriage, he appeared, wearing a brand-new blue great-coat and a hat, a gas mask slung from one shoulder, a cheap weekend case in his hand. She rushed forward and wrapped her arms around him, uncaring whether it was seemly or not.

'Oh, darling.'

Although he dropped the ghastly case and held her, he didn't seem as excited as he should be.

She pulled back, worried and puzzled.

'Darling, are you all right?'

'Yes. I am. I don't know why, but I've been spared.'

She suddenly understood, seeing in his face the tiredness and the guilt, at surviving when so many had not.

'Come along. Let's get you home, have a nice cup of tea.'

As they made their way out of the station entrance into the forecourt a civilian man going in suddenly spat at him.

'Bloody cowards, where were you?'

Rosemary was shocked rigid, but Biff kept walking, finding his handkerchief and wiping the spittle off his new coat.

She tried to look back but he pulled her along.

'It's nothing.'

'Biff — he just called you a coward, a

perfect stranger. What's it all about?'

He told her then. There was a lot of bad feeling against the air force. Why hadn't they protected the beaches? Where were they when the soldiers and sailors were dying in their hundreds?

Rosemary felt tears coming.

'But it's not *your* fault. You've been through hell as well, don't they realize that?'

He shook his head.

'Our contribution in the débâcle was useless — worse than useless. For all the bravery — and by God there were so many sacrifices — the bloody aircraft were useless. Men died doing their duty but with nothing to show for it. It was terrible.'

He shook his head.

'It's serious, Rose. The German war machine is . . . ' He winced, not wanting to say invincible, but that was what it looked like to him, 'so brilliant that if they ever get across the channel we'd be lost. The word is that Hugh Dowding is holding back all the Spitfires and Hurricanes he can to defend these shores, so he didn't waste any on us lot.'

Rosemary listened with a sinking heart. Things were even worse than she — and the general public — knew.

After a couple of days, something of the old Biff returned. They started to go to the pictures, though he tensed when newsreel shots of returning troops from Dunkirk were shown.

She got the long galvanized bath off an outside wall and put it before the fire in the sitting room. In the scullery she heated the water in the boiler used for the laundry.

Biff helped her ladle it into the bath. She went first, Biff soaping her back and shoulders, watching the suds slide down her breasts and over her nipples, her skin glowing in the flickering light of the fire.

Later, in their dressing-gowns, with mugs of tea and cigarettes, they listened as Winston Churchill's growling voice came from the wireless.

' . . . we shall defend our island, whatever the cost may be, we shall fight on the beaches, we shall fight on the landing grounds, we shall fight in the fields and in the streets, we shall fight in the hills, we shall never surrender . . . '

Rosemary had been upset when Italy had declared war on Britain on 11 June. The memory of all the lovely people she had met on her honeymoon was fresh in her mind as if it were yesterday.

As were Konrad and Anna.

She wondered what they were doing just then, what were they thinking after Germany had driven the British into the sea, and with the fall of France, the Nazis' rule of nearly all Europe. The sight of German troops marching through the Arc de Triomphe had been shocking, unbelievable.

What was Konrad doing in this awful, stupid war?

Had they changed? She discounted that with a snort of disgust for even thinking it in the first place.

Rosemary's thoughts turned to their plans to meet, and the date. They had said they would *definitely* make the 1 October, 1943. Surely everything would be resolved by then?

As the end of Biff's week drew closer they didn't go anywhere, just stayed together all day every day, walking the fields and estuaries, doing some gardening, simple everyday things. He helped her peg out the washing. At night they made love, sleeping until the dawn, then gently once again reaffirming the union of their flesh.

On the last morning he dressed once more in his uniform. She straightened his tie, and brushed the back of his tunic. He was now Flight Lieutenant Banks.

The time came to go to the station. He was being sent to a conversion unit on another type of aircraft — the twin-engined Wellington. Apparently strategic bombing was the next priority, after fighter strength.

Rosemary folded his greatcoat, ready to put it over his arm. The weather was far too hot for him to wear it.

'Are they safe, Biff?'

He tried to reassure her with a smile.

'Positively indestructible. They are built in a special way, something called geodetic, makes them very strong.'

She didn't look very convinced. She picked up his hat.

'Biff.'

He looked up, sensing something was coming.

'Yes, what is it?'

She took a deep breath.

'Biff, I can't go on like this, doing nothing, just waiting, waiting, waiting . . . *worrying* about you.'

Frowning, he prompted: 'So?'

Rosemary steeled herself and said:

'I'm joining one of the women's services. You don't mind, do you?'

'Which one?'

She swallowed. 'I didn't think it fair to be in the WAAF for obvious reasons; it could embarrass you. I'm reporting for training with the WRENS; they're recruiting at the moment.'

For a second Biff didn't know what to think. All he could say was 'When?'

Guiltily she winced.

'Next Monday. I report to Euston Station at 0 nine hundred hours.'

He just reached out and they hung on to each other. Over her shoulder he said: 'You take care now — no volunteering for anything hazardous.'

'Gosh, we don't do things like that, do we?' She sounded anxious.

He grinned. 'I mean working late with all those handsome naval officers.'

She gave him a playful slap, but her voice showed her concern.

'You sure you don't mind?'

He released her and stood back.

'Rosemary, I love you. I can see that being here with our world falling around our ears must be awful. You want to do something. I can understand that.'

She nodded. 'I do.'

'Fine.'

He waved his arms around. 'What are we going to do about this place?'

Rosemary sighed. 'I'd like to keep it if we can. It's our only home.'

He nodded.

'I agree.'

Somehow, the war had intruded further

into their lives, got a little more personal.

She went with him to the station.

He leant out of the carriage window, smiled.

'Now you be sure to write.'

The guard's whistle blasted out, answered by a toot from the engine and a surge of steam. Doors slammed as with a lurch the carriage moved forward.

He leaned out, she reached up and flung her arms around his neck. They had time for one good kiss, then she walked along the platform exchanging 'I love you's', miming the words as the train drew away.

She kept her eyes fixed on him, waving as he grew more and more indistinct, until the train lurched around a curve and he was no longer in sight.

Feeling lonely and frightened she made her way slowly back to the empty cottage. On the table was an envelope.

With fumbling hands she opened it.

Biff had written:

Darling, sometimes it's hard to say things without sounding silly, especially for a man — so I thought I would leave this with you. There is no use pretending that we do not live in dangerous times.

One day, please god never, I might not

come back. I just want you to know that I love you more than life itself. And if that terrible day ever does dawn please, please, always remember me as your loving husband, but don't let it ruin your life. I want to think of you as finding happiness again — and in whatever world it turns out to be, having a family and growing old with your children and grandchildren around you.

I fervently hope that it will be with me, but if not, and I am lucky enough to be flying again in those celestial clouds rather than stoking the fires of hell, I want to look down and enjoy your happiness.

Now, go and put this in the back of a drawer and forget my silly nonsense. It just had to be said.

With all my love,
Your husband

As if to lighten the contents he'd drawn a heart with an arrow through it, and 'B' loves 'R'.

As she read it tears dropped on to the paper, blurring the 'heart'.

13

He arrived at No 15 Operational Training Unit at Harwell, set near the meandering River Thames, with the Berkshire Downs in the distance, and the city of Oxford to the north.

As he was driven in a Hillman truck to the mess, he and the five others crammed in the back looked at the Wellington twin-engined bombers dotted all around the field, and in the hangars.

Since he'd known he was going on to the 'Wimpey' as it was affectionately called in the service, after the cartoon character of the same name in Popeye, he'd read a little about it. The airframe, designed by a man called Barnes Wallis, was of a peculiar geodetic construction and had apparently proved to be able to take considerable punishment. It was bigger than his Blenheim, and could carry eighteen 250-pound bombs.

They passed near one being worked on by the mechanics, its front turret with twin guns pointing starkly at the sky.

'Handsome bugger, ain't she?' somebody said.

Painted black underneath — after the ghastly losses of the daylight raids they were now a night-bomber force — and camouflaged on top, it did indeed look a very beautiful aeroplane.

Two days later he was climbing the short metal ladder under the nose and settling in the cockpit.

Beside him was Flight Sergeant Williams, his instructor, while sitting in their positions were his navigator, wireless operator and two air-gunners, all familiarizing themselves with their new tasks.

In the following two weeks they flew forty-two hours of instruction, practising single-engined flying and forced landings, instrument flying, and lastly progressing to formation-bombing practice, dropping dummy bombs at Odstone, and letting the gunners fire live rounds on the Aberystwyth range.

He was just on his final approach of the last day of his training when the radio broke in urgently.

'G for George, G for George. Break right — do not land — break right *now!*'

A red flare fired from the control tower hung brightly in the sky.

'What the hell . . . ?'

As they swung sharply away, pulling up the gear and with Biff ramming the throttles through the gate, the intercom crackled. It was the rear gunner.

'Skipper, there are Jerries right behind us, look like Dorniers.'

As if in a dream they had a ringside seat as the formation of enemy bombers passed serenely over the field. Great mounds of earth started to geyser into the sky, then a Wellington blew up in a ball of flame and black smoke. For a split second one of the hangars seemed to expand as if it was being inflated, before the windows blew out and it exploded, fire and smoke roaring up into the sky.

The formation flew on, and was gone as quickly as it had come. The sight of the crosses on the wings and the Nazi symbol on the tail fins were a shock. They were deep in rural England, not in France, not even in the south-east, where the great air battles were being fought.

But the *Luftwaffe*, as he later found out, had switched to attacking airfields in order to overpower the unexpectedly troublesome RAF.

They were ordered to stay airborne for a further twenty minutes, flying to a point near Cheltenham. If Harwell was ready they could fly back, otherwise they were to land at Staverton.

In the event they were ordered to return. From over thirty miles out they could see the black columns of smoke rising into the blue sky. When he eventually got down they taxied past squads of men fighting numerous fires. Four Wellingtons were still burning, as were several lorries.

The hangar had been blasted apart by the force of several explosions — not only those of the stick of bombs, but from the two aircraft inside that had blown up.

When he climbed down the short ladder he asked the corporal about casualties.

'Three dead, sir — all Waafs. A bomb scored a direct hit on their quarters, the bastards. Miracle was, the hangar was empty — they'd all been sent to the canteen.'

All Biff could think of was Rosemary. She might be in danger.

It didn't bear dwelling on.

★　★　★

Rosemary had reported to Euston Station, gathering with other girls as a smart Wren petty officer issued travel warrants and guided them to a train. It was three weeks after her medical and letter of acceptance, a week after Biff had gone back.

In one hand she carried her case which,

despite the restrictions on the list she'd been sent, was heavy with everything crammed into it that she thought she couldn't live without, including the two pairs of Navy-issue knickers that had been given to her at the recruiting office. She carried her gas mask with a strap across one shoulder, and her shoulder bag over the other. She was struggling up the platform when some Navy lads swooped on her, took the case and put her on the train before making off to join their unit which was forming up in the station yard.

The train was full of troops, so it was standing room only. She sat on her case.

People were sitting on the dirty floor all around her and in the compartments some were even lying on the luggage racks, but everybody was cheerful and helpful. Going to the lavatory was difficult, because it was also being used as a seat, with somebody on the floor under the basin. They struggled out as she struggled in, cracking jokes all the time, but she knew she was blushing.

Rosemary arrived along with the fresh intake at the basic training unit on the shores of Loch Lomond in Scotland on the following day, tired out, feeling dirty and wondering what on earth she had done.

The place was dreadful, full of Nissen huts

with deep waterlogged ditches between them.

They were starving, but all that was on offer was one sardine on hard toast which had been in the oven since breakfast two hours before.

It didn't get any better. There wasn't enough room for them, so for that night they had to get mattresses to put on the floor in one of the washrooms, stacking them against a wall. Several of the girls found them too difficult to carry on their own, so they all mucked in together — a first sign of what they would do in the years ahead.

In the afternoon they collected their free issue of basic uniform: greatcoat, gabardine raincoat, two suits, three shirts, collars and ties, and two pairs of shoes.

They were told that their pay would be twenty-four shillings per week, with a one-off grant of forty-eight shillings towards the purchase of further naval underclothes, and another pair of shoes worth thirteen shillings and sixpence.

They were also given thick navy lisle stockings, a hat, gloves and a housewife kit (called a hussif), containing needles, cotton, spare buttons and darning wool. There was much banter and talk of 'passion-killing' as they examined their two pairs of cotton pyjamas.

They were told that on no account were they to alter any of the items, a rule that was soon to be broken — girls were girls, after all.

They heard a bugle as they were sorting themselves out on the concrete floor, and a petty officer appeared in the doorway and ordered lights out. They scrambled to get into their beds before the petty officer threw the light switch, plunging them into near blackness, the only light coming through a small frosted window.

It seemed strange to be sleeping with so many girls, like being back at boarding school. As she tried to get to sleep she could hear somebody softly weeping into her pillow, just as she had done a decade before.

At 6.30 in the morning the door burst open and a piercing whistle was blown three times by the duty officer. Cold and half-asleep they scrambled to the washbasins. It was only then that they discovered that they had been sharing the floor with cockroaches, which scuttled away in the light. Later, they were to find that they shared their food with them too.

Assembled outside, they saw the other Wrens at divisions, looking smart in their uniforms, and they admired their straight-backed bearing, their precision marching and crisp saluting as the White Ensign was raised and the Royal Marines band played the National Anthem.

'How do they know what to wear?' Rosemary whispered to the leading Wren who had been assigned to look after them.

She nodded at a small flag on the mast.

'If the 'O' signal is at the top, wear raincoats; half-way and you carry them, and if there isn't one — it's no raincoats.'

Breakfast consisted of scrambled dried eggs that came out as if they were floating in water, one piece of bacon and piles of greyish-looking bread.

Six weeks of square-bashing followed, and when she wasn't doing that she scrubbed floors, cleaned basins, taps and lavatory bowls and prepared for kit inspections. Shoes had to be kept polished, especially the heel, and between the sole and heel under the shoe, and all buttons were to be shining and stockings darned if necessary.

They learnt that the floor was always called the deck, the bedroom a cabin, the kitchen the galley, a corridor a gangway, just as if they were on board a ship.

They were all called the ship's company.

Slowly at first, then with increasing confidence the squad drill improved, and soon they were marching in step, and swinging their arms up in rhythm, which seemed very hard work. But they were proud of themselves.

The stiff collars left red weals on their necks, and were painful until they toughened up — like their feet. Some people took longer than others to get the knack of tying their ties neatly.

One day they were marched to the ranges, and were instructed in rifle shooting. At first some of the girls were very anxious but Rosemary and one other had been allowed to shoot by their fathers. Seeing them do it settled the rest.

Lined up in the medical centre, arms already bared, the staff gave them their tetanus jabs with what seemed like very blunt needles.

It left Rosemary with a stiff arm for a couple of days.

Further training in protecting themselves in an emergency, and what to do in a gas attack followed, and always there was the scrubbing of floors, drilling, keeping fit and barrack inspections. Their blankets had to be removed from the bed and folded in a special way so that the last one wrapped around the other two, then placed tidily at the head of the bed on top of the pillow. All their kit including their tin hats had to be laid out as directed.

At last the day came for their passing-out

parade. Rosemary was the front marker, and as they passed the saluting base they all thought they were a very smart bunch indeed.

It gave them great satisfaction to see the dishevelled, disorientated new girls arriving, and to think they had been like that not all that long before.

Now they filed one at a time into the commandant's office to be given their postings.

The officer ran a pen down the list after Rosemary had given her number only.

'Banks?'

'Yes, ma'am.'

Satisfied that they had the right woman the officer said: 'You are going to be trained as a plotter.'

Rosemary had to suppress a nervous giggle. Was she to be parachuted into enemy territory to help plot things?

Instead she said; 'Thank you, ma'am,' took one step back, threw up a smart salute, did a sharp about turn, and left — to become a 'plotter'.

Outside, in the corridor, the giggles could no longer be contained.

★ ★ ★

Biff climbed nervously up the ladder in the gathering gloom, weighed down with his Mae

West and parachute, and carrying his bag with his Thermos and sandwiches. This was his first mission against the enemy since the terrible month of the battle of France.

He settled into the co-pilot's right-hand seat. It was policy for 'new boys' to have an experienced captain on the first couple of trips, just to keep an eye on things.

They went through the checks as the rest of the crew: the wireless operator, navigator and the two air-gunners settled in. At 10.00 hours that morning they had assembled at their flights, and had been selected for the night's operations.

Biff had then gone to his aircraft, and told the ground crew. Engines were run up, the wireless and guns checked and later 'G for George' would be bombed up with the ordnance detailed for the operation.

He had had lunch at the mess, and then reported to the briefing room at 14.00 hours.

When the CO had entered they all stood up, but he gestured for them to sit down again.

'Right, gentlemen, we're going back to Ostend. Give the invasion barges another pasting. First aircraft off at twenty-thirty hours will be F for Freddie.'

The order of the following crews had been given, and then other ops on that night were detailed.

After the CO the intelligence officer had briefed them on the aiming point, and given details of the known defences. Special target maps had been issued.

★　★　★

Biff started his engines and they went through the check list.

He wondered where Rosemary was, what she was doing, was she safe? The blitz was in full swing and Churchill had warned that German ships and barges continued to build up for the expected invasion.

They were given the signal to start moving out on to the perimeter track. His gloved hand eased the throttle levers forward, the aircraft shuddering and thumping as they passed over the concrete divisions.

The signals officer had notified them of the position of the airfield identification beacon which was situated eight miles from the runway and was moved each night to a different site. It flashed two letters of the morse code — different for each airfield.

Moving forward, he gently swung the tail from side to side to improve his forward view of the shaded lights guiding him out.

The signals officer also gave them the colours of the day: Very lights which they had to fire in the correct order when crossing the English coast on their return, to be reported by the Observer Corps.

They'd been warned: failure to get it right and they'd be fair game for their own fighters or anti-aircraft guns.

After the signals officer, had come the armoury man, who had briefed them on the bomb load, ordering the right mix of high explosive and incendiaries required for the target.

They reached the end of the runway and were held as the Wellington ahead of them, straining against its brakes, fiery exhaust from the nearest engine showing in the blackness of the night, finally started moving. Biff watched as the twin exhausts marked its path down the runway before it eventually lifted off and the burning points mingled with the stars until they were no longer visible.

He was given clearance to move into position and face the lights of the runway, but it would be several minutes before they would be allowed to go, to minimize the risk of collision.

He checked his fuel once more. The engineer officer had given them the allotted amount for the raid.

As he waited Biff looked again at the sky — clear and full of stars. The Met officer had given them the expected weather *en route*, over the target, and landing conditions on their return.

A single green light from the Aldis lamp on the roof of the control van shone out. It was time to go.

★ ★ ★

Rosemary had finished the 'plotters' course and had passed both oral and written exams, and with a sense of real achievement, used her hussif to sew on her dividers' badge.

Now she was being taken to a Glasgow station with two other Wrens, under naval escort, having been chosen for 'Special Duties' and having signed the Official Secrets Act.

It was nine o'clock at night.

'There we are, Jennies.'

The petty officer in charge used the nickname for the Wrens as he pulled back the compartment door. The girls struggled down the corridor with their kit.

'Afraid I've got to lock you in.'

When they complained he said: 'Orders are orders.'

'What about the . . . ' one of the girls coloured, 'you know . . . ?'

'Don't you worry, just give the window a

tap and we'll escort you.'

'Wonder what's so special about us?' said the last one in as the door was slid shut and locked.

It was a troop train, and not long afterwards the platform filled with marching columns of men with full kit and rifles. There was a lot of stamping of boots, then they started boarding with all their equipment. Several tried the door as the carriage became chock-a-block, and the Navy petty officer motioned for them to lower the blinds, which they did.

The journey was long and was interrupted by innumerable stoppages for bomb-damaged lines ahead, sometimes they were shunted into sidings to let other trains pass.

The only dim light they had was from the one blue bulb allowed during the blackout, too dim to read anything by.

The journey went on and on, with nothing to eat or drink except the bottle of water and one round of corned-beef sandwiches that they'd been issued with.

When daylight broke at last they couldn't see much of the outside because of the glued-on anti-splinter net on the window. After several more hours they slowed down and lurched over lots of points. Through the small triangular area left clear on the window, taking it in turns, they could only see marshalling yards and a fog of dust that hung in the air. A smell of burning came into the carriage.

'Wherever we are, they've had a pasting last night,' observed Rosemary when it was her turn to have a look out.

At eleven o'clock they found themselves on the platform in Liverpool. Rosemary was separated from the others, they all waved goodbye and went off to get their transport.

She was put on another train, this time without a locked reserved compartment, and had to endure another four hours sitting on her case until they pulled into Euston.

But her travels were not over.

Twenty-five hours after she had left Glasgow she found herself at Great Yarmouth, reporting to the Royal Naval Barracks: HMS *Skirmisher*. After that, Rosemary had to walk around the corner to the Victoria Hotel which was the WRNS quarters. Sandbags were piled half-way up the bay windows. She found she was sharing a cabin with several others. They seemed a jolly lot.

Her first watch was at 6 a.m. in the morning, lasting until midnight. She accepted a cup of something called Kye, which turned out to be a block of unsweetened chocolate with water, and boiled until thick. Evaporated milk was added, and sugar.

When she sipped it she found it had a really greasy texture, but it warmed her up and by the time she'd finished it her hunger seemed to have disappeared.

Her night's sleep was broken by an air-raid warning. In the shelters they listened to the throb-throb of the German planes, but no bombs came down; they were presumably on their way to the Midlands.

She wondered about Biff. Was he going in the opposite direction at that very moment? She said a little prayer for his safety.

★ ★ ★

It was his third trip, his first as captain. A new fresh-faced young pilot officer sat on his right; the whole cockpit was lit up with intense whiteness by a searchlight. They were at 7,000 feet, flying straight and level on their bomb run, with heavy flak coming up all around them. Every now and then the Wellington gave a vicious jerk. *Something* was hitting them, but all the controls felt normal.

As soon as the navigator operating the Mark Nine bomb-sight decided they had reached the predetermined position on the two parallel wires, the bombs were released with a 'Bombs away'.

They all knew it was a pretty inaccurate business, so it was absolutely essential to remain straight and level, and the German gunners knew that.

Biff immediately broke away, engines roaring, plunging into the safety of darkness, and turning for home. The weaving searchlights frantically searched the heavens, but they never found them again.

The tail gunner noted with satisfaction the fires starting down below.

On the return journey everybody kept a track of where they were by observations. After crossing the Dutch coast they strained for a feature in the East Anglian coastline that would help the navigator plot a course for home. It came from the front gunner.

'Looks like Southwold down there, sir.'

It was.

Ten minutes further on they saw the red beacon flashing its Morse code, and later, the green light that told them that it was safe to land.

Biff brought her down on the runway passing over the gooseneck flare: a lit two-gallon water-can fitted with paraffin and a wick, and then between the two rows of twelve glim lamps that marked the runway's borders.

When they had taxied to their dispersal point, and finally switched off the engines, the quietness was startling. He was so stiff that he could hardly get down the ladder. His muscles had been tensed up for hours.

Next morning the ground crew set about patching the fuselage and wings where shrapnel from the bursting flak had ripped through the fabric. Almost all the aircraft on the squadron were far from their pristine best: oil-stained and patched from continuous operations.

★　★　★

It was sometime before they could meet — briefly — in London. Biff strained his eyes to see her coming off her train at Liverpool Street station, but she was right up to him laughing and holding up her arms before he recognized her in her navy-blue uniform and hat.

They rushed at each other. Biff swung her round. When, after many moments he set her down, they searched each other's faces, not speaking. Suddenly she cupped his face and kissed him tenderly.

'Darling, I've missed you so much.'

Conscious that they were both in uniform, he still kissed her back, long and passionately. Several times in the past few weeks he'd wondered if he'd ever see her again.

Arm in arm they walked out of the station and got on the underground.

'Where are we going?'

Rosemary was wondering, hoping, she so wanted to be alone with him.

He gave her a squeeze.

'I've got the use of a flat. Belongs to a chum's auntie.'

The tube was crowded, so they were crammed close together, strap-hanging on the Central line all the way to Lancaster Gate. It was early evening, but already people were bagging their spaces and bunks for the night's stay on the platform seeking safety from the nightly air-raids.

When they came out above ground, it was to find people running towards their entrance, some with children in tow, and air-raid sirens wailing.

He looked at her quizzically.

'Would you prefer to stay here until it's all over?'

She took a deep breath.

'How far is the flat?'

Biff shrugged. 'Three minutes' walking — two if we run.'

'Let's brave it then.'

Hand in hand they ran down the street of Edwardian stucco-walled mansions and red-brick flats. The streets were rapidly emptying, and they could already see searchights criss-crossing the night sky, and hear the sound of explosions — probably the anti-aircraft guns in Green and Hyde Parks. The nightly blitz was at its height. Back in August Winston Churchill had given his now famous speech, saying of the RAF: 'Never in the field of human conflict was so much owed by so many to so few.'

Yet the terrible sacrifice of men in Bomber Command, especially in Number Two Group was largely unknown to the public.

He let her go, searching for the keys as she surveyed the portico with its Greek-style columns flanking the heavy door.

'Very nice.'

He looked up, then led the way up the steps.

'It was grand once, but it's four flats now, one on each floor.'

Theirs was at the top, in what was once the maid's quarters. He opened the door, switched on the light — then had to run to the window to pull the blackout curtains.

Rosemary let her shoulder bag slide down on to a sofa that faced a fireplace with a gas fire now set in the hearth and looked around. It wasn't plush, but it was reasonably furnished with a couple of easy chairs, a coffee table with copies of the *Illustrated*

London News, Picture Post, *Punch* and other magazines. There was a standard lamp in the corner. There were some pictures on the walls and, on a shelf that ran around the walls at picture-rail height, about fifteen large decorative plates.

'Here's the kitchen. Like a cup of tea or something?'

'Ooh, I'd love one.'

He filled the kettle, put it on the top of the gas cooker and lit a ring.

'I'll put on the fire.'

In the sitting-room he squatted down, and turned the tap. By the time he'd got a match alight and put it to the bars, there was a 'whump' as the coal gas ignited with a lick of flame.

Rosemary stood over him, chuckling.

Biff looked at her slim legs encased in black stockings. When she leant down and offered her hand to haul him up he dragged her down on top of him.

In a frenzy they kissed and struggled with their clothing. Eventually Biff stood up, his braces around his waist, picked her up in her navy-blue petticoat and carried her into the cold bedroom, flicking the door shut behind him with his foot, so plunging the bedroom into darkness.

They were oblivious to the kettle's whistle,

to the sound of bombs and gunfire as he drove into her with a savage animal desire, as if his body knew that he was living a dangerous life, that there was an urgent need to pass on his genetic material to continue his bloodline before it was too late.

A bomb whistled and exploded somewhere near, shaking the building, making streams of dust drop from the ceiling. There was a sound of plates smashing in the sitting-room.

Through the window the sky was continually alive with brilliant flashes of light, and the outline of the building opposite was enhanced by a huge redness behind it that grew and grew. As, at last, he could do no more in his animal union with this woman whom he loved and lusted after, he held on to her and took her with him as he fell to the floor, making sure he took the fall, then rolling her under the high bed as the shrill scream of a bomb grew louder and louder.

14

The whole building seemed to lift from the ground and then drop down again. The window blew in, the door came off its hinges the curtains were torn from their fixings. The room was full of a fog so dense that in the dark they couldn't see more than a foot in front of their faces.

Coughing and spluttering they held on to each other and felt their way into the blackened sitting room. He flicked the switch but there was no light, and the gas fire had gone out.

'Ouch.' He trod on the kettle which rolled unseen on the débris-covered floor. 'Hang on while I get my shoes.'

Outside the shrill sound of alarm bells told them that fire engines and ambulances were arriving in the street.

'It must have been bloody close.'

He found his shoes and crunched back to her, then carried her to the sofa and left her to dress.

Still coughing he pulled apart the curtains and looked down into the road.

Two fire engines and an LCC Daimler

ambulance were on the tarmac made wet by leaking hoses now snaking out of sight. He couldn't see the house that had been hit: it was about three doors up round a slight bend.

'I wonder if we can do anything?'

Even as they watched, another ambulance arrived and shadowy figures wrapped in blankets, seen by the light from fires and by intense flashes that lit up the whole street, were helped into the back. Some were on stretchers.

In the dark, holding hands, they had to pick their way carefully down the flights of stairs, but eventually they made it to the road.

Where a house they had passed less than an hour ago had once stood since 1910 there was nothing but a huge pile of wreckage. Next door, on either side, were exposed rooms, the flowery wallpaper and black fireplaces now obscenely on the outside.

A crowd of men, some in Auxiliary Fire Service uniform and steel helmets, others in blue boiler suits were working frenziedly, tunnelling into the mound of wreckage which was ablaze at the back. The hoses were being played on it, the spray soaking the teams of men. Up the street a broken gas main was sending flames over a hundred feet into the air.

Biff found a man who was directing operations.

'Anything we can do?'

The man took in their uniforms.

'Not this time, sir, thank you. Luckily we've got a good team on the job.'

He nodded at the bomb-site.

'Don't know how many are in there, but our information is that a family of four lived in the basement.'

At that moment a vicious whine made them all duck.

'Bloody shrapnel — from our own ack-ack. Sorry, miss.'

He turned away as shouting came from the rescue workers. A woman was being dragged out, face and body blackened, half-naked from the effects of the blast. She was placed on a stretcher and rushed to the open doors of an ambulance.

They turned and retraced their steps.

It was too dark to do anything about tidying up. There was no electricity, no gas, no water.

They went back to bed, blindly shaking and slapping the dust and plaster lumps off it, cuddling up, talking, catching up, interrupted by bangs and crashes. Rosemary tensed up every time, until, still in each other's arms, they went to sleep as the world outside slowly calmed and peace reigned once more.

In the morning they were woken by a couple of pigeons, cooing loudly on the paneless windowsill.

Biff sat up, licking his dry lips, as Rosemary stirred beside him. He looked down at her, and started to laugh.

Rosemary's eyes opened wide even as she frowned.

'What's funny?'

Then she too began to laugh.

They were both covered in a white dust from the plaster that had settled, unseen in the dark of the night, on to the bed. Now, with their pink lips and white hair they looked like clowns.

The hot tap gave only enough cold water from the tank in the eaves to wash their faces and bodies, and the cold one only dribbled, and petered out with the kettle still only two-thirds full.

In any case there was no gas.

He turned to the drinks cabinet.

'I can offer you a whisky and soda, a dry martini, a — '

'Ugh.' Disgust showed on her face. 'Stop, you're make me feel sick.'

He straightened up.

'Right — we're going out for breakfast.'

She gestured at the room with her hands

widespread. 'But what about this mess?'

He found her coat, gave it a shake.

'Breakfast first, then we'll get down to it.'

★ ★ ★

The pain had gone. He felt so much better. He raised a hand to his head, felt his eyes, moved a leg. Yes, everything seemed good, but why was he lying on the bathroom floor? Had he fallen? He rolled slowly on to his side, and then on to his front. Maybe it was the bomb. Carefully he pushed down on his hands and tried raising himself. He was very weak, but he managed to get shakily on to all fours. His body felt as if he had gone ten rounds with Joe Louis. He crawled towards the toilet, needed it to get into a kneeling position. He winced with the hardness of the tiles on his skinny frame. He waited for a while, fighting to get his breath back, then he got to his feet, half-falling against the cistern. He grabbed at it, then moved slowly along, holding on to cupboards until he reached the door. He pushed it wide open. She wasn't there, the bed was rumpled but the room was intact. And then he realized: it was a modern bedroom — it wasn't the war. It was the year 2007.

That dreadful time was long gone.

Whatever had made him think of it?

Then he remembered what he had been doing that day. He'd been to the high sheriff's . . .

He shook his head. Maybe it was the sight of that laid-up RAF colour, or the rays of light falling on to the woman sitting on her own at the front of the church? They had brought so many memories flooding back.

He made it to the bed, crawled in under the duvet, shivering now. Biff pulled it up over his head to get warm, he was so cold.

★ ★ ★

It was the altitude he realized, the four-engined Halifax was at a much higher ceiling than in the early days on the 'Blimps.' Flying at 18,000 feet and with draughts like rods of ice blasting in it was appallingly cold.

They flew in layered silk, wool, and leather, but still shivered. Regularly his sandwiches froze solid — even the scalding-hot coffee became a cold drink after five or six hours.

He was on his second tour now in 1943, and everything had changed as he had changed. With the increasing number of aircraft deployed — tonight there were over 728 — raids had to be streamed, and Pathfinders — special squadrons with the top navigators aboard, went ahead to drop flares over the target.

Tonight it was Hamburg, especially the docks.

Two minutes before the zero hour at 1 a.m., twenty of the Pathfinders had dropped yellow target indicators blind on H2S — the centromeric radar system. Hamburg's river and coastline gave the city an excellent, sharp image.

Eight more Pathfinders carrying red TIs aimed visually, and then a further fifty-three backed them up with green flares.

Now the order had been given to the main bomber force, of which he was one, to attack from zero plus two minutes to zero plus forty-eight, and to overshoot the markers by two seconds in an effort to reduce the 'creepback' which had dogged recent attacks. His mind drifted back to earlier in the day, to the briefing which was so much more detailed, crowded, and busier than in the early days.

He'd flown an air test on his Halifax that morning, the ground crew going along as tradition demanded.

In the mess they had gathered around the wireless with their drinks to listen to the one o'clock news in complete silence.

Last night a force of three hundred and ninety aircraft of Bomber Command attacked the German Naval installations at Kiel

Some scant details followed, then:

Six of our aircraft are missing.

When the wireless was switched off they had resumed talking again, but minds remained for a while on those six crews.

Lunch was followed by the briefing.

All those listed on the battle order of the day, often over a hundred men, assembled in the briefing room, sitting as crews together. The chatting had stopped as the squadron commander entered, with the navigation officer, the intelligence officer and the station commander. They all stood but the station commander motioned them to sit down again.

Maps were displayed, with pinned ribbons showing the route and the return course, which was different, followed by short pithy descriptions of the nature of the target, take-off times, the size of the attacking force and order of battle, and bombing heights.

A second large map covered with clear celluloid detailed with crayons the known enemy defences, flak concentrations, and now, different from the early days when they were non-existent, the night-fighter danger zones.

'Met' had followed with details of the weather *en route* and over the target, and then the navigation officer gave the turning points, the crew navigators scribbling hard to get it right. It was vital, since in the dark they could not see other aircraft.

The take-off time had been given, and they had then ambled out of the smoke-filled rooms to call at the intelligence unit to collect a small pack of escape items, containing silk printed maps, energizing sweets, stimulants, a small compass, and money for use in Holland, Belgium or France.

The next few hours of anticipation and growing anxiety would drag on. Biff had actually gone to the camp cinema, watching without actually taking in George Formby strumming his ukulele and rushing around in some sort of comedy.

The Halifax was much bigger than the Wellington. He had got out of the transport and walked under the huge black shape, several times the size of a double-decker bus, with its nose pointing at the heavens.

Inside, as he had settled into the left-hand seat of the cramped cockpit, the distinctive smell of oil, metal and leather of the Halifax assailed his nostrils.

He had glanced down as usual through the perspex hood at the ground crew with their mobile battery — known as the trolley acc, waiting to start the engines.

He'd followed the usual drill with his flight engineer.

'*Ground/Flight switch — set on ground; throttles set; pitch — fully fine and locked; supercharger — medium gear — radiator shutters open.*

Fuel tanks selected and booster pumps on.

Ignition.

Contact.'

As each of the four Merlin engines roared into life, the ground crew scurried about under the wings, disconnecting the external battery leads and removing chocks from beneath the huge wheels, each as high as a man.

The heavily laden Halifax had needed a long run on full throttle before, gradually, its tail had risen and he had coaxed it reluctantly into the air, climbing slowly away with throttles locked on.

Now, as they made for the target in darkness, there were unseen bombers all around them. Above and below were more aircraft, yet, except when they hit the slipstream of another aircraft, they could have been all alone in the night sky, isolated even more by the steady, deafening roar of the four Merlin engines.

'Green TIs ahead, skipper.'

He came back to the present, the here and now of the continuous war the RAF had been waging for the last three and a quarter years against Nazi Germany.

He flicked his mike switch.

'Thanks, bomb-aimer. I see them.'

The radio crackled again.

'Master bomber to all aircraft, bomb the red markers; I say again, bomb the red markers.'

They'd been to the target before, on 24 July when the use of 'window' for the first time had completely fooled the German air defences.

It had been the most massive attack of the war by Bomber Command.

And now, in quick succession they were attacking it again, with a force nearly as big, and he felt a deep unease.

He was carrying five tons of bombs to the city where Konrad and Anna lived.

It was ironic to think that in a few months' time they were supposed to meet — and now he was doing his best to kill them.

He could only pray that they were no longer living there.

The bomb-aimer, lying in the nose, now

took over, directing Biff towards the aiming point. Silent against the roar of the engines, heavy flak burst around them in red angry flashes, which swept past at great speed.

Flares dropped by night fighters hung above them. A sudden brilliant flash marked the end of a Halifax.

Through the intercom the bomb-aimer gave Biff continuing guidance.

'Right. Right. Le . . . ft. Steady . . . '

Searchlights, normally radar-guided, tonight seemed to be aimlessly raking the night sky; then suddenly, just ahead and beneath him, were the red target indicators.

He held the aircraft dead steady. Seconds passed. He glanced out through the side of the plexiglass and was suddenly transfixed with horror.

Even as he watched his ears crackled with: 'Bombs gone.'

The aircraft leapt into the air. He fought to steady it for a further twenty seconds until a photo-flash went off to record the bomb bursts.

But it was hardly needed. What had horrified him now became apparent to them all as he dropped the nose and banked away to gain speed and get out of the target area as fast as possible.

In silence they watched as below them a

huge firestorm was raging, engulfing what seemed to be miles of streets; hurricanes of flame and smoke were tearing through the heart of Hamburg at incredible speed.

The black silhouettes of hundreds of aircraft slid in silent formation over the inferno. The searchlights criss-crossing the sky from the edges, suddenly covered one of the black crosses. Tracer and flak bursts were everywhere — all without sound. Only the deafening roar of their own engines filled their ears.

They'd never seen the battle group bombing over the target before.

As well as the flares and bomb bursts, marked by beads of intense light that expanded in an instant to the horizon, sudden eruptions of flame — like pictures he'd seen of solar flares, reached up from the seething swirling sea of fire as houses and factories exploded in the heat.

There could be no doubt; if Anna was down there she must be dead.

It affected him deeply.

When they were well over one hundred miles from the target area the rear gunner said the sky was still red raw behind them.

He was thankful that he wasn't in the battle order for the final raid on the city.

When the intelligence reports filtered

through a month later the figures were truly staggering.

Twenty-two square kilometres of the city had been engulfed in the fantastic firestorm. It was reckoned that 42,000 had died, and a million refugees had left the city. Over 40,000 houses had been destroyed, and a quarter of a million flats, and well over 5,000 factories. But it was the 277 schools that got to him, albeit they were empty at night, and the twenty-four hospitals that were probably not. It began to haunt him.

Shaken, Biff went to see the CO. He was told to take a seat and was offered a cigarette. The 'boss' noticed the slight tremor in the hand of the young pilot, who looked older than his record card indicated. He'd checked: Banks had been on operations for two whole tours now and had won a DFC.

'What's on your mind, Biff?'

He could guess what was coming. The man had come to the end of his tether, wanted to be permanently stood down. It happened two or three times a month. It was a serious matter, and he'd developed a strategy to deal with it, like all Bomber Commanders.

Biff swallowed, took a deep breath.

'I can't go on in Bomber Command sir — that raid on Hamburg . . . ' he shook his head sadly, 'I had German friends there

271

— met them before the war. I just can't do something like that again — ever.'

The CO nodded, aware of the horrific damage and loss of life — more than the Luftwaffe had managed in the entire blitz on Britain. He cleared his throat.

'I can quite understand. I do hope your friends are all right. What I think you need is a break — a training squadron for a while. Of course, no CO can promise never to send you there again; it would set a precedent.'

Biff shook his head.

'No, you misunderstand, sir. I can't continue on *Bombers* — I just *can't* — ever.'

The CO sat back.

So he was refusing to serve — was in danger of having his papers stamped LMF — 'lack of moral fibre'. It would damn him for the rest of his life.

He became less sympathetic, his face darkening.

'Now that's enough, Banks. You realize if you take this any further you could get into really hot water. It's a bloody serious thing to say.'

He tried to lighten things as he continued: 'I see from your record you've been on 'ops' almost continuously except for the conversion course to Halifaxes. I think you need a spot of extended leave. Do you the world of good.'

Biff suddenly realized what the CO was thinking.

'No sir, you don't understand. I want to fly still — and *fight* for my country; it's just that . . . ' he hesitated, 'I don't want to bomb civilians any more. I can't.'

He shook his head violently.

The CO looked puzzled. 'What do you want? Because I doubt whether with your multi-engined experience you can get on to fighters now.'

Biff had given it some thought before taking the momentous step of seeing the CO.

'I realized that sir, so what with the Battle of the Atlantic and all, I wondered if you might put me up for a transfer to Coastal Command. There is a pretty fierce war being fought by the Banff Wing, I believe.'

Frowning, the CO scratched his chin.

This was a new one for him. Bomber Command was the one branch of the service that was actually attacking Germany, taking the war to the enemy. They were fêted now like the fighter boys in 1940, except perhaps by the locals who lived near the bases. There had been some pretty contemptible goings on: resentment about airmen hogging the local facilities; wives and girlfriends who lodged in the nearby villages were often treated with ill-concealed disdain, as if they

273

were scarlet women from the cities. Yet the locals went to bed in safety as every night his boys went out to do battle. Most nights you might get away with no casualties, other nights a couple of crews didn't return — or even more. It was heartbreaking. He had to write the letters to wives and mothers.

He glanced down at the file.

'I see your wife is in the WRNS. Has that got anything to do with this? You know you'd be unlikely to find yourself any nearer to her than you are now — wherever she is.'

Resignedly Biff shook his head again.

'No, it's nothing to do with that, sir. I can't do my job any more and that's not fair on my crew, or you and the squadron — or me.'

The CO ran his eye over Biff's record again, and realized that the fellow had been lucky, had done an above average number of ops, especially if you included the early days.

Funnily enough, he'd met a 'coastal-type' last time he'd been at the Air Ministry. Perhaps that had been a sign? He'd give him a ring.

He made a snap decision.

'Go and see the MO, have a word in confidence, get him to give you the once-over. Meanwhile — no promises — but I'll investigate the possibilities of a posting to Coastal. Of course, it depends on their needs,

I can do no more than that — otherwise you've got to soldier on. Understood?'

Biff was dismissed. He got gratefully to his feet, put his cap on, saluted and left.

When he was gone the CO ran a weary hand over his forehead. Why was he bothering with Flight Lieutenant Banks when there was so many other pressing things on his mind?

But the U-boat menace was still with them, sinking hundreds of tons of shipping. He'd give it a try. Coastal Command was considered the Cinderella service; Bomber Command got priority in everything. He put these thoughts aside and got on with planning the night's raid.

★ ★ ★

Rosemary had come up into the open after finishing her night watch, the Ops and plotting room was protected well below ground.

When she'd gone on duty the previous night, walking along the front, she had heard, beyond the barbed wire defences, the crashing of the waves on the shingle beach, had dimly seen the white foam in the dark.

It had been busy in E-Boat Alley, the horizon was lit by the flashing of guns as convoys ran the gauntlet of torpedoes and bombs from the Luftwaffe.

Further down the coast, at Lowestoft, she knew the MG and MT boats would be waiting to sally forth to the rescue.

And above it all, before she had reached the sentries guarding the sandbagged opening, had been the steady roar of wave after wave of unseen RAF bombers heading east — towards Germany.

Tears had come into her eyes before she got a grip of herself. Biff was up there somewhere, if not that night then tomorrow, or the night after that.

Every morning, as now, she dreaded a call to see the commanding officer. The air was cool, damp, the sea and sky an unremitting grey. There were hardly any waves; the sea was very calm.

She stepped out briskly. Rosemary was now a leading Wren with one anchor, known as a hook, sewn on to one arm. Their hats had been changed to sailor-style, which was much more comfortable. Anxiously she scanned the louring clouds — just in case. Several times she had been shot at as she had marched with others, by low-flying German aircraft. Once they had dived for cover under a bench seat put there in the days of peace for people to sit looking out to sea, enjoying themselves.

She was walking fast to get to their

quarters first — there was only sufficient hot water for about four baths.

When she got there she rushed upstairs, bagged the bath and turned on the hot tap to fill it to the level of the line painted on its inside at five inches deep.

While that happened she peeled off her uniform, stripped, and had a good wash everywhere at the hand basin before enjoying the quick luxury of a soak, leaving the water relatively clean for two other girls from her watch.

Sometimes they were beaten to it and there was only cold water; and sometimes there was no coke, so no hot water at all for anyone.

The Salvation Army or the YWCA would occasionally be able to offer an alternative, but it usually meant a very quick cold bath — very *very* quick in the freezing depths of winter.

Dead beat, she turned in, wondering whether there would be a letter from Biff by the time she woke up.

There was.

He was having two weeks' leave in a few days' time. That was unexpected and immediately she worried as to why. There had been no mention of it in his last letter.

She would put in for leave straight away to coincide with his, if not wholly, then partly.

She began a letter to him. They hadn't seen each other since two days spent together in the spring. All that time the cottage had stood empty.

Still waiting for an answer to her application, Rosemary was washing her smalls in a hand basin, rubbing them with a big block of soap, rinsing them several times but still finding them coated with a scum from the hard water. She was just stringing them up to dry in the bathroom, when the air-raid siren started up.

Quickly she tripped downstairs to the basement, grabbing her tin hat from its hook. She'd just joined the others when a huge explosion rocked the building. The lights went out leaving them in total blackness. Some of the girls screamed and started to cry.

One of their petty officers called out: 'It's all right, it's all right. Stay calm.'

A torch came on, then another.

They were all covered in dust, and the door was jammed. They were trapped, but they could already hear shouts and the sound of work going on. Reassured, they knew it was only a matter of time before the Navy would get them out.

Eventually the door was dragged open, and the first gulp of fresh air she took was marvellous, as was the mug of hot, sweet tea.

The nearby barracks had received a direct hit, and there were many dead, including a Wren officer and six Wrens, but the girls on duty in the underground ops and plotting rooms were safe.

A fire started, and Rosemary, part of a chain, helped to pass buckets from a standpipe. Her only loss were her smalls, which were nowhere to be seen — nor was the wall on one side of the rubble-strewn bathroom. In the confusion of requartering in the town — which was possible because nearly all the civilians had been evacuated at the start of the war, and because of the memorial service to their dead comrades, it was several days before she was given permission for a week's leave on compassionate grounds.

Because Biff and she were a married couple in the services, she was given priority, though many others were being sent home for a few days, suffering from shock and minor injuries.

But there was a further order, one that took her completely by surprise. Afterwards she was to report to 'Coppins', a royal house which was an officer-training camp for WRNS.

On arriving home, Rosemary started to walk from the station, but some friendly Americans pulled up in a Jeep and gave her a ride all the way to the front gate of the cottage.

As she walked up the path the door opened and Biff came out to meet her. She dropped her case, flew into his arms and started crying. Rosemary kept saying sorry, but it took some time for her to calm down.

He was dressed in a cardigan and flannels — so wonderful to see, bringing back memories of happier times.

But he was different: she knew it almost immediately. It was not his face, which looked strained, and she could see more lines radiating out from the corner of his eyes. It was his manner. He didn't seem to have the vigour of old.

'Darling, is everything all right?'

They were sitting around the fire he'd got going as soon as he had arrived; the cottage was very musty and damp.

He smiled and shook his head.

'I can't go on.' He continued shaking his head. 'I can't go on bombing any more, Rosemary.'

He told her then about Hamburg, and what he'd seen and subsequently heard.

She bit her lip.

'Oh God. Konrad and Anna?'

He nodded. 'I know.'

There was a silence, only broken by the

crackle and popping of the flames in the grate and the settling of lumps of coal as they burnt away.

She looked very worried, eventually asked miserably:

'What's to happen, Biff?'

He didn't look at her, using the poker to stir the fire and add a couple of lumps of coal before sitting back again. 'I've asked the CO for a transfer.'

In truth she was torn between relief that perhaps he wouldn't be over Germany every night in the thick of it — she was only too well aware of the attrition rate, and worry that he was going to do something foolish. Then she immediately chided herself. What was more important, for God's sake: the safety of her husband, or her pride?

'Transfer to what, Biff?'

He told her then what he had asked for.

Rosemary blinked. It was not what she expected.

'Do you think you'll get it?'

'I don't know. How is the war at sea going?'

She shrugged.

'Better than for a long time, but the U-boats are still sinking an awful lot of our ships.' Rosemary frowned. 'I shouldn't tell you this, I suppose, but Jerry's got a new device called a schnorkel. Apparently they can charge their batteries without coming to the surface. People are very worried about it.'

She got up and came and sat on the side of his chair, and put her arm around him, kissing the top of his head, smelling again the masculine freshness of his hair.

'Whatever happens, don't you worry, Biff. We'll always be together.'

She completely forgot to tell him about her news, that she was to train as an officer, only remembering when they were in bed that night. For the first time he gave a chuckle, as of old.

'So, I'm going to bed with a fellow officer. We'll both be cashiered.'

Over the next couple of days, he did seem to be getting brighter. They went to the pictures, dodging, in the dark streets, buses and the odd taxi with their dim, masked headlights, and groping through the 'light lock' to enter the cinema, only to be dazzled by light and noise.

Afterwards they treated themselves to fish and chips, with lashings of salt and vinegar, deciding not to eat them as they walked home, which would have cost one shilling and eleven pence, but to stay in the chip shop, and have bread and margarine, and a cup of tea, all for two and sixpence.

On these occasions she'd 'tarted' herself

up, had altered some of her pre-war dresses — shortening them, and, as stockings were unobtainable, she'd stained her legs with brown colouring, and got Biff to draw a nice straight pencil line down the back for a seam, slapping his hand away as it wandered further than it should have.

Several times they went to the pub — he for a quiet pint, Rosemary sipping a small glass of cider. For him it was different from the mess where, often as not, it ended up with some excitement: great choruses of *Do you know the Muffin Man* as they tiptoed one by one across the floor with pints of beer on their heads, or 'walked' with sooted feet on the ceiling, having reached there by way of a great pile of mess furniture, singing: *You'll get no promotion this side of the ocean* . . . So it was nice to find a snug corner amongst all the copper and brassware, and talk sweet nothings. Until one night.

A boisterous crowd of Americans came in, jostling and whistling at some of the girls with their English boyfriends, who looked bleakly back. Some army lads arrived, and took up a position at the other end of the bar. The noise in the place greatly increased. Biff and Rosemary finished their drinks, then looked at each other. At the unspoken question in his eyes as he held up his empty glass, she murmured sleepily:

'No, let's go home.'

They stood up. As she edged her way through the crowd of Americans they ignored him, smiling and wisecracking as they let her past, making sure she had to brush against them. Biff was annoyed, but they were a long way from home, and were brothers in arms. And in any case, you made allowances — they were so brash and different in attitude and manners from what they were all used to.

But then one large crew-cut sergeant blocked her path, stepping to one side and then the other as she tried to pass.

She smiled. 'Excuse me.'

The sergeant leered. 'Any time, honey.'

'I'd like to get by, please.'

Biff was slightly behind, elbowing his way through the others, who were already reforming behind her, whistling and nudging each other. Biff only realized what was happening when the man said:

'Well now, that's going to cost you a little kiss, sweetie.'

Biff roughly pushed the last man aside and reached her as a large hand came round her waist and pulled her in against the sergeant's barrel chest. As he leant down to kiss her Rosemary twisted to one side.

'No! how dare you.'

284

Biff's hand gripped the sergeant's fingers and yanked them back, pulling the hand away.

'Leave my wife alone.'

Beneath the crew-cut the square face went black with anger.

'Stay out of this, buddy.'

Biff shook his head.

'No, *you* get out of the way.'

'Whoa.' The sergeant looked around for support.

'You hear this little limey, will ya?'

He turned back to Biff, leering.

'You guys over here are all pantywaists, needed us to come and win the war for you.'

Grinning at everybody he said:

'So what are you going to do about it?'

Incensed as he was, Biff bit down on his teeth and, pushing Rosemary, started to get past.

The Yank grabbed his arm and swung him around. Biff saw the pile-driver coming a mile off. He swayed back out of its path and stepped in to punch the big face with a straight left, carrying all the weight of his body behind it.

The man took down three of his buddies who tried to break his fall, but the others jumped on Biff, and the army lads charged at the same time like a row of Rugby forwards piling into the scrum.

Girls screamed, glasses were thrown, blood shot from mouths and noses. Biff somehow got out from under a pile of bodies, stopping only to help the sergeant up, then hitting him again with such force that a tooth came flying out of his mouth. He crashed back to the floor and rolled over, all sixteen stone. He would only come round after the Snowdrops and Redcaps had barged in, quelling the warring sides with truncheons, night-sticks, and, quite unofficially, pickaxe handles.

By that time Biff, holding on to Rosemary's hand, was legging it up the street.

She gasped: 'Biff, *now* I can understand why they call you that.' It must have been the adrenaline rush, but there was an animal heat in them both.

Up an alleyway, he lifted her up and she swung her legs around him. Held by him against the wall, Rosemary pulled her knickers aside and guided him in. It was all over in a couple of minutes.

They continued on their way in silence, as the realization of what they had just done sunk in, leaving them shaken and ashamed.

Before the war such behaviour, even the thought of it, would have horrified them both.

But the straitlaced society of the 1930s was

coming apart in the shared danger and the close proximity of young men and women away from home, and with the arrival of the Yanks with their easier ways.

Not that they thought they would ever join the ranks of such lewd behaviour: after all, they had a home to go to.

Ruefully Biff worked his bruised hand and bit his lip.

'Sorry, that was unforgivable, I don't know what came over me.'

Rosemary clung to him.

'Or me, Biff. It takes two, don't forget.'

She gave an embarrassed giggle.

'Anyway, I enjoyed it, but my back is killing me.'

The days passed easily; they got up late, stayed up late, walked, rode — they hired a couple of bony nags, and Rosemary's riding-breeches, smelling of damp, were replaced by a pair of bell bottoms she'd thrown into her case at the last moment for work around the house.

The last whole day dawned.

Rosemary was in the kitchen when he came down the steep narrow stairs, ducking his head under the low doorframe. The smell of fried bacon filled the room.

'What's this?'

She turned when she heard him.

'I'm using the last of our rations — there won't be time tomorrow morning.'

He nodded.

He would be seeing her to the bus, off to become an officer. Biff had another couple of days.

'There.' She placed the plate on the table before him turning back to get hers, using a tea towel to hold the hot plates.

They sat down, didn't speak as he sprinkled salt on the fried egg — fresh ones from the farm where they went riding.

At last he said: 'What shall we do today?'

Rosemary thought for a moment.

'Biff, I'd like it if we just spent time around here — together.'

Which is what they did — cleaning, dusting, beating the carpets over the line in the back yard, even painting, using some tins from under the stairs which he'd put there in 1939. He cleaned the brushes outside, then came in to find Rosemary using a flatiron heated on the range, pressing her white shirt.

A pile of ironed clothes was on the end of the table.

'There — that's done.'

He put the brushes back under the stairs, and washed his hands in the sink.

They both knew that this studious domesticity was to cover the impending heartbreak of being separated again.

And for how long this time?

They'd got a chicken from the farmer, and some vegetables, and she'd baked an apple pie. Biff had found three bottles of red wine when he'd rummaged around looking for the paint. He'd already opened one. It wasn't bad.

Rosemary dressed for the occasion, and Biff did his best to look smart.

With the chicken on the table, and the vegetables steaming in their serving dishes, he poured her a glass of wine, then did his own.

When all was ready they clinked their glasses.

Biff said: 'To us.'

Rosemary responded:

'To us.'

When the meal was finished, he opened another bottle, and took it into the sitting room. Rosemary was in her favourite place of old, in front of the fire sitting on the floor, back to the sofa. Dance music was playing softly on the wireless.

He refilled her glass, then settled down beside her.

There didn't seem to be any need to say anything, but eventually Rosemary murmured:

'This bloody war has ruined everything, hasn't it, Biff?'

He took several seconds to answer.
'Yes.'

She took a sip of her wine. He noticed that Rosemary seemed to have difficulty swallowing. She turned her head away from the fire and faced him.

'Do you realize that it will soon be the first of October again?'

He nodded, adding as if to underline what she had said. 'Nineteen forty-three.'

She looked back at the grate.

'Yes. It's all so sad isn't it?'

The fire crackled and snapped, spitting out an ember.

He flicked it quickly back, sucked at his fingers.

Her voice was resigned.

'Do you think we'll ever see them again, Biff?'

He shrugged his shoulders.

'I don't know. Perhaps October 'forty-eight — if this war is over by then.'

But as he stared into the depths of the fire, the awful memory of the Hamburg raid came back to him.

That night they didn't make love, just held each other in their arms, whispering, remembering, all those people they had known before the war; all the young people from school and the tennis clubs, and the parties. Where were they now? How many were still alive?

And inevitably they reminisced about the glorious days of their honeymoon, with Konrad and Anna in Sorrento. For a while they lapsed into silence at the memory. Neither wanted to sleep — to waste their last hours together, but of course they did, drifting off around two o'clock.

The alarm, set for 5.30, sounded like a fire bell. His swatting hand hit the plunger and the clock, knocking it off the cabinet.

They stumbled around, getting ready. Biff made a cup of tea, then helped her get her case down the stairs.

It was a twenty-minute walk in the fresh morning air. It had rained in the night. There was a small group huddled around the bus stop. They stood to one side, whispering out of earshot.

'Take care now, darling.'

He smiled.

'I will — and you — you go and be a good officer now.'

They lapsed into silence. With their arms wrapped around each other there didn't seem anything else to say.

At last the bus showed around the bend, and braked to a halt. The waiting queue shuffled aboard, passing down the lower gangway or scuttling up the curved metal staircase.

Biff got her suitcase into the luggage area beneath the stairs and faced her on the platform.

She fought back tears, gave him a quick kiss as the conductor called out:

'Hold tight.'

With a double ring and a crunch of gears the vehicle jerked forward.

With that Biff swung off the platform and stood in the middle of the road.

She remained where she was, waving, but he couldn't see her for very long; the dim blue bulbs and the anti-blast net on the windows meant that the inside was almost invisible after twenty yards in the gloom.

He waved anyway, until the bus was out of sight.

15

Biff felt the pain coming back, knifing into his returning consciousness. And he needed to go to the lavatory again.

Clenching his teeth and holding his chest he got to the edge of the bed, rested there for a while, then the urgency to wee got too much.

Shakily he rose to his feet and, stumbling, made for the doorway. He could see the outlines of things, the dawn must be coming up.

Biff reached for the light cord, missed, and fell for the second time. He went down and hit the tiled floor hard, screaming out in pain.

The snapping sound of a shoulder bone was like a pistol shot.

On the cold floor he couldn't help whimpering like an animal. He tried, but couldn't reach the alarm button, the thing had twisted around his neck.

He called out.

'Darling, help me. Darling — help me.'

After what seemed like hours the coldness around his lower body turned warm, and crept up to his shoulder and the pain began to ease.

* ★ ★ ★

He realized he was drifting in his dinghy. He must have used the last of the morphine shots. His mouth and lips felt like leather, cracked and dried. There was no more drinking water. It wouldn't be long now . . .

The second, and last pass of the Halifax over the U-boat had settled both their fates.

Even as he had straddled it with a stick of Torpex-filled depth charges, the eighty-eight mm flak cannon mounted behind the conning tower had ripped through the cockpit, killing his copilot instantly, and splattering him with blood and bits of tissue. Fire was raging in one engine and in the root of the other wing near a fuel tank.

It was only a matter of time before the Halifax blew up.

Down below in the blackness was the icy water off the coast of Norway.

It would be a miracle . . .

He fought the controls, keeping her as steady as possible.

They'd left Stornoway in the Outer Hebrides at midnight, and after hours of patrolling the icy waters his operator had reported a contact on the ASV radar screen.

Guided on to the target, Biff had switched on his Leigh light mounted under the port wing. The twenty-four inch, fifty-million candle-power carbon arc searchlight had sent a concentrated beam of light flaring downward.

And there, still a shock, caught starkly in the harsh pool of light, was a U-boat on the surface, the muddy grey water foaming white around its shadowy hull.

He'd gone straight into the attack, but the anti-aircraft armament of the U-boats at this stage of the war was formidable. On the first pass at fifty feet the starboard engine had exploded in flame and black smoke.

But their stick of Torpex-filled depth charges fused to go off five seconds later at a depth of twenty-five feet, must have severely damaged the U-boat because there was no attempt at a crash dive.

The tracer fire had increased as they came around again, his gunners engaging in a fierce firefight.

As they passed over it, releasing a further stick of charges, there had been another explosion, and the Halifax had leapt in the air. He knew it was a mortal wound, the elevators were badly damaged. The plane became almost uncontrollable.

He thrust the throttles full on, fought to gain height, ordered the crew out.

They protested but he shouted over the

radio: 'Go-go-go. I can't hold her much longer.'

The navigator struggled up to him, looking wildly at the body of the co-pilot.

'Sir, we could lash up the column, you could just make it . . . '

Biff shook his head.

'It won't work. I'm barely holding her — go on — drop the survival boat and get out while you can. Go.'

A hand patted him on the shoulder.

'See you in the mess, skipper.'

Freezing moist air blasted in through the fuselage as the hatch was released.

He waited as long as he could, then lost the struggle and began to lose height, going down in shallow circles.

He thought of Rosemary, and the life they would never have together. Dawn was just breaking, he could see the horizon but it was all black down below — until he saw the red glare.

As he drew lower he suddenly realized what it was: the U-boat on fire.

Biff knew he had little chance — ditching at night in an ice-cold sea that was running white horses — he'd seen them in the Leigh light.

So there was no real decision to be made. Here was one of the enemy that they had spent hours, days, months, criss-crossing grey empty oceans to find. An enemy that had sent millions of tons of shipping, with the loss of weapons, fuel and above all food to the bottom; had nearly brought Britain to its knees, and had killed so many sailors, drowning with oil-choked lungs in cold oceans with no known grave, or burnt to nothing in the enormous fires of burning tankers. He was only doing his job. Sweating with the effort, at fifty feet he levelled out and aimed for the conning tower. At the last moment he could see men running around on the flame-lit deck. Tracer came at him from fore and aft, whipping soundlessly by, sometimes hitting the fuselage with a sound like gravel thrown at a dustbin. As the bridge filled the forward view he saw what must have been the captain standing upright, unflinching as the final act of their lives was played out with terrifying speed.

Just as the blazing Halifax came in, a huge explosion in the U-boat lifted her out of the water, breaking her back. The Halifax's flaming wing sheered off as it struck the conning tower, the rest of the aircraft went spinning violently into the sea, breaking into hundreds of pieces.

From their dinghy the three survivors of the Halifax 'C for Charlie' could only see scores of little fires on the oily water about a mile away.

The wireless operator had managed to signal their attack as they went in. With a bit of luck the search and rescue boys would get to them that morning, and if the sea calmed they might even get a Sunderland from Sullen Voe setting down to pick them up; they could be in the bar, sinking a pint of 'heavy' by the evening.

But they didn't talk much, they were in shock, and the motion of the enclosed rubber boat was making them sick.

As they clung on to the handles, facing each other, the white-faced navigator said: 'He ought to get the top gong.'

'Posthumous' muttered somebody.

★　★　★

He came to when the cold water closed over his head. Choking, he fought back to the surface, helped by the inflated Mae West. He thrashed wildly around, then went under again as a green wave rolled past. When he came up he grabbed at a dark shape that seemed almost to lift off the top of the waves, catching the wind. As soon as his hands found the rope loops on the rubber he realized it was a dinghy, and from its size and shape, a German one — from the U-boat.

He knew he had to get into it *now*, or he'd die very soon in the freezing water. It could only be a matter of minutes and then he wouldn't have the strength.

With his first attempt he found his right arm was useless, and pain reverberated all over his chest.

He held on grimly, as wave after wave washed by. It dawned on him that roughly every fifth or sixth one was bigger, more powerful.

He knew he had the strength for only one more attempt — then he might as well let go and finish it sooner rather than later.

As soon as a large wave roared past he started counting and manoeuvring around so that the next would push him in the right direction. He began psyching himself up.

He heard it coming, hissing as it broke on the crest. As the powerful wave lifted him, he propelled himself up, and clawing with his good arm, rolled into the rubbery embrace of the dinghy — and right on to a body.

As Biff scrambled away in horror he realized, even in the dark, that the man was dead.

He was colder than the sea, colder than the air, cold as only the way a dead body can be.

Biff settled in the opposite corner, away

from it, seeing only the dark bulk against the lighter outline of the stars.

The pain in his arm and chest, out of the embrace of the water, made him cry out in agony. Fumbling with his one good hand, he managed to pull out his survival kit from a thigh pocket. Just by the feel of its contents he found the morphine stick, pulled the cap off with his teeth, and stuck it into his thigh through a rip in the material.

As the pain lifted he drifted off into unconsciousness.

It was the squeaking and screaming of gulls that eventually brought him round. His body was stiff, and there was violent pain every time he moved his right arm: it felt broken. To begin with his eyes were stuck together. He had actually to use his fingers to prise one open, and then the brilliance of the daylight momentarily blinded him.

When he managed to take in his surroundings, it was to find he was all alone on a very calm, sunlit ocean.

The birds screamed again — and then he realized what they were doing: pecking at the face of the dead German opposite.

His mouth and throat were swollen and dry, unable to produce the shout he had intended. Instead only a hoarse croak escaped from his grossly swollen and cracked lips.

He swung his good arm, kicked out with a leg, scaring the birds off.

His eyes turned to the German's head. Weirdly, it still had its cap on and the face possessed a large, but well-cut beard.

It was only then that he realized he had come face to face with his enemy: it was the captain of the U-boat.

Biff stared and stared. It was the first time in the long years of the war that he had ever been so close to any German before — the enemy had never been seen.

The face was swollen and black with blood and oil. There was a huge gash in the man's side and lines of congealed blood: he had bled to death. Thick oil was caked in his beard.

It was a slow process — the recognition.

It wasn't just any German.

It was Konrad.

16

The rest of the crew had been picked up hours earlier by a Sunderland that they had so dreamed of.

But the air-sea-rescue launch that had also been dispatched to the area decided to do one last box search in the fading light of the day.

One of the look-outs sweeping the horizon with binoculars suddenly stiffened, called the bridge.

'Something off the starboard side, sir.'

As they approached, it was quite dark and they switched on the searchlight.

'Looks like two dead Jerries, sir.'

But as they came alongside, the man sitting behind the other, arms wrapped around nursing him, moved one arm to shield his eyes from the harsh light.

A shout went up.

'One of them is alive, sir.'

Two of the crew went down the scrambling nets and held the dinghy steady as another stepped carefully into it. Suddenly he turned and yelled up at the bridge:

'Christ, sir, he's British — looks like the pilot.'

In the small sick bay the orderly diagnosed a broken arm, dehydration and delirium. They wrapped blankets around his blue, shaking body.

'He keeps on saying sorry, sir.'

The duffel-coated captain frowned. 'Who to?'

'The dead Jerry, sir. He went crazy until we brought his body aboard. It's the U-boat skipper.'

As the needle went in, peace came over Biff at last, the peace of chemical nothingness.

It could not last for ever.

★ ★ ★

On the bathroom floor Biff made no attempt to struggle. An inner warmth had come over him. He knew, like the old wounded animal he was, that this was the end. Mother nature was about to return him to the dust he'd risen from all those years ago — in another world now long since gone.

And it was time he went, as well.

His mind kept drifting from the present to that other world.

★ ★ ★

They'd put him up for another gong, and the powers that be had taken their time agonizing about it. In the end it was approved, but before he had been gazetted he made it perfectly plain: he would not present himself for the award, would not accept it and would send it back if they awarded it. He could not live with the idea that he was being fêted for something that had led to the death of his friend.

At one time in the dinghy he'd talked to Konrad for hours, asking why they hadn't written, and how was Anna? Once, sure that Konrad's eyelids had moved, he'd grabbed his lapel with his good hand, and had shaken him violently, before collapsing back in tears.

He had been treated in hospital in Stornoway, then flown to the mainland and taken to a lovely country house just outside Aberdeen, which had been requisitioned as a convalescent home. Rosemary had been notified and granted immediate leave to see him.

She'd passed her officer course and had been sent to Norfolk House, St James's Square, working with the naval section on the plans for the invasion of occupied Europe.

She was in a huge room with maps covering the walls, sometimes attending chief of staff's conferences in the morning, other times overseeing the sorting of all the postcards of Normandy, maps, Michelin

Guides and photographs that the public had been asked to send in under the guise of a general war effort.

Some postcards of beaches began to be pinned to the walls in several rooms. She was living in a nurses' hotel, travelling on the tube every morning, then walking down the Haymarket with the surging crowds.

In the April of 1944 she moved to Southwark House with the naval unit. They were accommodated in Nissen huts, set in a large area of parkland, but worked in the main house. It was the Supreme Headquarters, Allied Expeditionary Force — SHAEF for short, and she saw them all — General Eisenhower (Ike), Montgomery, even on one occasion Churchill.

As the date for the invasion drew nearer they sometimes worked eighteen-hour days, only stopping to don tin hats as the air raids came over thick and fast.

She hadn't seen Biff since that week they'd enjoyed together. From his letters she knew he was now with Coastal Command. They began tentatively to talk of the future. Although the war was far from over, there were signs at last that it might end one day in the not too distant future.

On the night of 5 June 1944 she and all the others didn't go to bed; they knew that the order had been given for the assault on Fortress Europe to be launched in the early hours of the new day. They heard the sound of the paratroopers' planes going over. All the girls felt very emotional at what might happen.

A month later Rosemary and a contingent of WRNS crossed the Channel themselves, the ship's Tannoy blaring out, over and over again, Bing Crosby singing: 'Would you like to swing on a star'.

She'd transferred on to a landing craft before setting foot in France for the first time since her honeymoon six long years before. As they travelled behind the advancing army, under the umbrella of SHAEF, troops would wave and wolf whistle and the girls waved back. They had been found quarters in the ruined city of Caen when the next-of-kin message had come through. Biff had been reported missing in action. Rosemary read it again, couldn't take it in, then felt weak and slumped down into a chair. She was given immediate compassionate leave and flown by Dakota to Northolt. All the way, as far as the eye could see through the little window, the Channel was still full of hundreds of ships. She prayed over and over again for a miracle.

And her prayers were answered.

Good news awaited her.

He'd been found, suffering from exposure and with a non-life-threatening wound. She was to go to a transit unit who would issue her a travel warrant for Aberdeen.

She was bursting with happiness as she got off the underground.

★ ★ ★

He had made a special effort, with the help of the nurses, to look really spruce for her, with a new uniform, a sharp shave, teeth brushed, and a clean sling.

He was in the lounge, gazing down the drive in anticipation of the first sight of her as she got out of her taxi.

A car did turn up the drive — a staff car. A wing commander and an RAF chaplain got out, looking up at the house as they tugged at their uniforms. They looked very serious.

As they made their way to the front door he had a sudden, awful premonition. He'd never had one before.

He heard their hushed voices in the hall, and the sound of the door opening behind him. He stood, utterly still, willing it not to happen, but then a hand touched him gently on the shoulder. He couldn't turn, his body was frozen.

'Squadron Leader Banks?'

He didn't want to say yes. He *didn't* say yes, but the voice continued anyway.

'I'm sorry. I have some very bad news. Perhaps you'd like to sit down?'

No, he *didn't* want to sit down, *didn't* want to hear as the voice, after a long pause, murmured very quietly: 'I regret to inform you that your wife, First Officer Rosemary Banks, was killed today by enemy action . . . '

At last the voice faltered: 'A V1 . . . '

The world stopped then, had no meaning, no time, no existence.

17

If he had died she perhaps wouldn't have been at that place at that precise time. He should have died, not her. Was this God's punishment for killing Konrad?

But he *was* dead of course. Maybe he was breathing still, eating, sitting in the grounds, always watched, but his heart was dead.

★ ★ ★

Biff turned on his back, knew that the time had come. As the last of the blood coursed through the arteries of his brain, the images became intense, vivid.

★ ★ ★

He'd returned to the damp musty loneliness of the cottage a couple of months after the war in Europe ended, discharged early on medical grounds.

As soon as he heard that the cottage had not been re-let, he'd wanted to go back there, eventually getting the estate agent on the phone after several hours of trying.

'Of course,' said the man, 'nothing would give us greater pleasure than to see you back with us. By the way, I think the owners would like to sell it. Would you and Mrs Banks be interested?'

Biff said nothing, other than that he'd like it for six months, then perhaps . . .

'And how is Mrs Banks? Is she still in the WRNS?'

Of course, he had to tell him then, heard his voice going mechanically through the routine, and the aftermath of accepting kind condolences. He'd done it so often.

'Such a tragedy — a lovely lady, lovely.'

He could imagine the man at the other end shaking his head.

As the war was finally over, and crowds were celebrating VJ day, he'd sat in front of the fire — summer or not — with a bottle of whisky, and one of her blouses, pressing his face into it, catching the last vestiges of her scent, and crying, drinking and crying until oblivion mercifully came.

He contemplated suicide. He'd kept a German Luger revolver and a few rounds: a trophy of war — of death. He was drinking and looking at it, loaded and ready on the table beside him, remembering all he could of their short life together, and Sorrento, when he suddenly, thought of Anna. Was she alive?

310

Did Konrad have children? Should he get in touch with her? The Allied Commission or the Red Cross presumably could come up with the answer, and an address.

Then he thought of what he'd say to her: that he had been the one who . . .

He shook his head sadly. No, he was alone now, all alone. He'd only stir up trouble and pain for her and for himself.

But he didn't have the guts even to pull the trigger. It fell from his shaking hands to the stone floor, and fired. The bullet whined as it ricocheted around the room. He stood rock-still, hoping. But it ended up in the oak beam above his head.

He slumped back into the chair, face in his hands, and wept.

The year passed, and another, meaningless, without aim, without feeling.

He'd got a job with a seed merchant of all things, but it suited him to be alone all day in his car as he toured the farms of East Anglia, some around airfields he'd flown from.

Already the control towers were crumbling, the glass panes smashed, the metalwork twisted and rusty, the runways pushing up weeds.

A good thing really, but somehow sad. So many young men in their prime . . .

And already the atmosphere of those war

days was changing, people were not helping each other out as they once had.

Sometimes by these decaying airfields, as he ate his sandwiches and sipped coffee from his Thermos flask he thought he could hear singing — men's voices raised in rousing choruses: 'Bye bye blackbird, You'll get no promotion this side of the ocean . . . '

Sitting there, watching the end of the harvest, with the stubble in the fields, the rooks circling in the trees near a church, and the fading signs of the war that had taken the love of his life, there was only loneliness: the coming autumn of shortening days would only bring more tears.

He knew he couldn't go on like this. He made his mind up.

Later that day he made enquiries, found he could fly direct to Naples by the new British European Airways. After that it would be by the train again. But the thought came to him that, of course, he needn't get return fares, he wasn't going to come back. So he'd treat himself to a taxi all the way to Sorrento.

Thomas Cook made all the arrangements. Biff drew the necessary money from the bank, and counted out on the desk the large white fivers as he paid the bill.

A week later he looked around the cottage for the last time. It looked dead to him now, cold, empty — *dead*. He'd had a good clear-out of their stuff, even finding his letter to her in case of his . . .

He'd balled it up and put it on the fire, watching it burn.

He locked the door behind him, and dropped the keys into the estate agent on the way past. The rent was paid up to the end of the following month, but he explained he'd definitely left now, wouldn't be coming back. They wished him well, assuming he was moving away.

The journey was uneventful, the air hostesses looked after him very well in their smart new uniforms. They landed at a military airfield near Naples and after a bit of haggling he found a taxi that would take him all the way to Sorrento.

He was saddened to see the bomb damage in Naples, especially near the docks. As they drew nearer to Sorrento he began to get tense, but the place looked the same, albeit more run down, with rubbish blowing in the street; but there was no great damage, it was just emptier and poorer, like everywhere else in the world.

When the taxi turned into the drive of the hotel he braced himself for change. The gardens were overgrown, a jungle.

But there, when it came into view, was the

hotel they'd come to for their honeymoon, a little run down, with peeling paint and green mould growing on one wall.

The reception was shabby, the floors scuffed by heavy army boots, and the lovely woodwork of the desk was dull and chipped.

Behind it, a young girl smiled shyly at him.

He'd specifically asked for their room. Following the aged porter he was full of trepidation, praying it would be the same. It was almost ten years to the day.

'*Signore.*'

The man led the way in. He needn't have worried. A part from a few cracks in the walls — probably caused by the bombing, and a general feeling of neglect, it was the same, a faded time capsule that he could wrap around himself.

His heart was heavy. It would do just right. He felt sorry for the hotel and its staff, struggling to get back on its feet after such appalling times, but it was something that he had to do — was going to do this time, where they had been so happy.

When he was alone he unpacked, taking the Luger from its cosy place between his shirts.

Biff went out on to the balcony. One of the Roman busts was missing, but the view was exactly the same, with Vesuvius, smoothly rising above Naples Bay to his right.

The little harbour wasn't so busy, but in all other respects it was the same, nothing was different, except that *everything* was different.

He dressed for dinner, but the dining-room was only sparsely occupied, and only a few were in black tie. Gone were the richly dressed people, dancing to the orchestras, leaders in white tuxedos.

But to him it *was* a special night, the night he would join her, so he had a bottle of the finest red, a local one, a good one, a good *year*, nineteen thirty-eight.

Afterwards he went out on to the terrace, lit a cigarette. There wasn't a moon, but the millions of stars were twinkling above a dark, unseen, but lapping ocean; the Milky Way glimmered like a bright band directly over his head.

He only became aware of a figure standing near him as he turned to leave, to go up to his room — *their* room.

The woman was in deep shadow, standing between the light coming from the two open french windows.

She was unmoving, had been for some time.

At last she moved, came out of the shadow.

Still they didn't speak.

She was as beautiful as ever, but there were

many threads of grey running in the dark hair.

And she looked tired, drawn, her eyes seemed bigger with the leanness of her face.

Without speaking they drew nearer, stood for an eternity searching each other's face.

Slowly they reached out, put their arms around each other, and just held on.

It was Anna.

★ ★ ★

Biff died, his face set in a smile.

18

The funeral took place at the same church where the high sheriff's service had been some two weeks before.

It was 2.15 when the organist stopped playing Bach's *Jesu Joy of Man's Desiring* and the packed congregation stood as his coffin was brought in, escorted by the clergy and carried on the shoulders of the bearers, to be laid before the altar.

Slowly the family filled the two front rows of reserved pews.

They remained standing, and sang the hymn: '*Be Thou My Vision, O Lord of my heart*'.

Prayers followed, then his son, Conrad, climbed the pulpit to deliver a tribute to his father. A woman whispered how like his father he looked.

Conrad Banks surveyed the sea of expectant faces, took his time.

'All of you knew my father in one way or another, from business, or the Rotary Club, or from the many charities he worked for, or indeed the Office of High Sheriff.'

He paused, checked his notes before looking up again.

'But I wonder how many of you know of his earlier days, as a pilot in the war. He rarely spoke about that part of his life, or the fact that he was married before he met . . . ' his eyes found his sister, 'our mother.'

Conrad looked back at them all.

'She was called Rosemary, and both my father and mother made quite sure we knew of her existence, she was never forgotten in our household.

'Tragically, she was killed during the war serving in the WRNS, one of a total of over three hundred young girls killed in the service of their country in that branch alone.'

Conrad Banks paused, shuffled the cards on which he had written his notes.

He placed his hands on both sides of the lectern, and looked serious, defiant even.

'We were equally made aware that Mother had also been married before, in Germany, and that her first husband, too, was killed in action, unbelievably against Father, in one of those weird coincidences that life throws up. Even more remarkably, Mother forgave our father, a testament to the bond of friendship that had been forged, by chance, before the war. And of course, testament to her loving and forgiving nature, and the fact that she and father found love again, with each other. Like so many of their generation, they had to pick themselves up and start all over again.'

He smiled. 'I'm very glad they did, as my sister and I wouldn't be here today if they hadn't.'

There was laughter. It didn't seem inappropriate, not at Biff's funeral.

Conrad waited before continuing.

'Biff and Anna celebrated their diamond wedding anniversary not long before she, sadly, passed away. She spoke such beautiful English that some people never realized her origins.

'Mother had a wicked sense of humour, and many of you will remember the beautiful woman who stood beside her husband in his shrieval year — an Anglo Saxon office, as she never let him forget.'

Conrad became grave, looked a bit hesitant, nervously cleared his throat.

'Thanks to the Freedom of Information Act and my sister,' he smiled, 'Rosemary, being such a wizard with computers, we uncovered an amazing fact that we have since had verified by the Archive Records branch of the Royal Air Force.

'We wondered about mentioning it today, but in the end we decided we would, as a footnote to his life, and history.

'Biff was cited for a medal for his part in the sinking of a U-boat; in fact, it's no exaggeration to say that the Victoria Cross was being considered.'

There was a stirring in the congregation. He gave them time to settle.

'It became clear that my father refused all medals to do with the incident — which, of course, led to the death of Anna's husband, and after the war he worked tirelessly, with Mother, for the promotion of friendship and understanding between Germany and Great Britain.'

When he'd finished, Conrad resumed his seat. Prayers of thanksgiving and intercession followed, including the Lord's Prayer, before, dark-haired and strikingly like her mother, Rosemary mounted into the pulpit and opened her Bible.

She coughed and then explained.

'A reading from the RAF Bible, as used in Coastal Command during the war: Chapter Seven, psalm sixty nine, verses one to three.'

She cleared her throat.

'Save me God, for the waters have come up to my neck
I sink in deep mire, whence there is no foothold
To have come into deep waters, and the flood sweeps over me
I am crying, my throat is parched.

My eyes grow dim with waiting for my god.'

Fighting back tears she stepped down and returned to join the family, hands comforting her as she sat.

His coffin was preceded down the aisle to the door by a piper playing a lament.

The final chapter in the lives of Biff and Anna, Rosemary and Konrad was over.

A generation was passing into history.

We do hope that you have enjoyed reading this large print book.

Did you know that all of our titles are available for purchase?

We publish a wide range of high quality large print books including:
Romances, Mysteries, Classics
General Fiction
Non Fiction and Westerns

Special interest titles available in large print are:
The Little Oxford Dictionary
Music Book
Song Book
Hymn Book
Service Book

Also available from us courtesy of Oxford University Press:
Young Readers' Dictionary
(large print edition)
Young Readers' Thesaurus
(large print edition)

For further information or a free brochure, please contact us at:
Ulverscroft Large Print Books Ltd.,
The Green, Bradgate Road, Anstey,
Leicester, LE7 7FU, England.
Tel: (00 44) **0116 236 4325**
Fax: (00 44) **0116 234 0205**

Other titles published by
The House of Ulverscroft:

CHILDREN OF THE REVOLUTION

Dinaw Mengestu

Sepha Stephanos owns a newsagent and general store in a rundown Washington, D.C. neighbourhood. Seventeen years ago he fled the Ethiopian revolution after his father was killed. His life now is quiet, serving the few customers he has. Every Thursday evening is spent with his two friends; they talk, joke and drink whisky. When a white woman named Judith moves next door with her mixed-race daughter Naomi, Sepha's life seems on the verge of change. His fragile relationship with them gives him a painful glimpse into the life he could have lived and for which he still holds out hope.

THE WELL-TEMPERED CLAVIER

William Coles

A schoolboy at Eton College, with not a girl in sight, seventeen-year-old Kim's head is full of the Falklands War and a possible army career . . . until the day he hears his new piano teacher, the beautiful but pained India, playing Bach's *Well-Tempered Clavier*. Kim's life is destined never to be the same again. A passionate affair develops and he wallows in the unaccustomed thrill of first love. Twenty-five years on, Kim recalls that heady summer and how their relationship was so brutally snuffed out — finished off by his enemies, by the constraints of Eton, and by his own withering jealousy.

1	21	41	61	81	101	121	141	161	181
2	22	42	62	82	102	122	142	162	182
3	23	43	63	83	103	123	143	163	183
4	24	44	64	84	104	124	144	164	184
5	25	45	65	85	105	125	145	165	185
6	26	46	66	86	106	126	146	166	186
7	27	47	67	87	107	127	147	167	187
8	28	48	68	88	108	128	148	168	188
9	29	49	69	89	109	129	149	169	189
10	30	50	70	90	110	130	150	170	190
11	31	51	71	91	111	131	151	171	191
12	32	52	72	92	112	132	152	172	192
13	33	53	73	93	113	133	153	173	193
14	34	54	74	94	114	134	154	174	194
15	35	55	75	95	115	135	155	175	195
16	36	56	76	96	116	136	156	176	196
17	37	57	77	97	117	137	157	177	197
18	38	58	78	98	118	138	158	178	198
19	39	59	79	99	119	139	159	179	199
20	40	60	80	100	120	140	160	180	200

201	221	241	261	281	301	321	341	361	381
202	222	242	262	282	302	322	342	362	382
203	223	243	263	283	303	323	343	363	383
204	224	244	264	284	304	324	344	364	384
205	225	245	265	285	305	325	345	365	385
206	226	246	266	286	306	326	346	366	386
207	227	247	267	287	307	327	347	367	387
208	228	248	268	288	308	328	348	368	388
209	229	249	269	289	309	329	349	369	389
210	230	250	270	290	310	330	350	370	390
211	231	251	271	291	311	331	351	371	391
212	232	252	272	292	312	332	352	372	392
213	233	253	273	293	313	333	353	373	393
214	234	254	274	294	314	334	354	374	394
215	235	255	275	295	315	335	355	375	395
216	236	256	276	296	316	336	356	376	396
217	237	257	277	297	317	337	357	377	397
218	238	258	278	298	318	338	358	378	398
219	239	259	279	299	319	339	359	379	399
220	240	260	280	300	320	340	360	380	400

401	406	411	416	421	426	431	436	441	446
402	407	412	417	422	427	432	437	442	447
403	408	413	418	423	428	433	438	443	448
404	409	414	419	424	429	434	439	444	449
405	410	415	420	425	430	435	440	445	450